AMITY

MICOL OSTOW

EGMONT

NEW YORK

EGMONT
We bring stories to life

First published by Egmont USA, 2014
443 Park Avenue South, Suite 806
New York, NY 10016

1 3 5 7 9 8 6 4 2

www.egmontusa.com
www.micolostow.com

Library of Congress Cataloging-in-Publication Data
Ostow, Micol.
Amity / Micol Ostow.
pages   cm
Summary: Two teens narrate the terrifying days and nights they spend
living in a house of horrors.
ISBN 978-1-60684-156-3 (hardcover) — ISBN 978-1-60684-380-2 (eBook)
[1. Haunted houses—Fiction. 2. Supernatural—Fiction. 3. Brothers and sisters—
Fiction. 4. Family life—New England—Fiction. 5. Moving, Household—Fiction.
6. New England—Fiction. 7. Horror stories.] I. Title.
PZ7.O8475Ami 2014
[Fic—dc23
2013041535

Printed in the United States of America

For Mom, Mazzy, and Lawsy—

three fearless broads

It was night, and the rain fell; and, falling, it was rain, but, having fallen, it was blood.

—Edgar Allan Poe, *Silence: A Fable*

PROLOGUE

HERE

Here is a house; bones of beam and joints of hardware, stone foundation smooth, solid as the core of the earth, nestled, pressed, cold and flat and dank against the hard-packed soil and all of its squirming secrets.

Here is a house; sturdy on its cornerstones, shutters spread wide, windowpanes winking against the speckled prisms of daylight. Weather-beaten slats of knotted siding, drinking in nightfall. Tarred shingles surveying star maps, legends shared in the pattern of dotted constellations above.

Here is a house; not sane, not sentient, but potent, poisonous, drenched with decay.

Here is a house of ruin and rage, of death and deliverance, seated atop countless nameless unspoken souls.

Here is a house of vengeance and power, land laid claim by

3

*wraiths and ciphers, persistent and insistent, branded and
bonded and bound.*

Here is where I live, not living.

Here is always mine.

NOW

Dear Jules:

The Halls moved out of Amity today.

She told me. Amity did.

Like a bat out of hell. Or bats, I guess, seeing as it was the four of them—Mr. and Mrs., and the kids, Luke and Gwen. Who aren't really kids, you know, with Gwen being exactly my age— our age—and Luke barely a full year older. Not quite twins—not like us. But close enough, right?

Anyway: Gwen. I could tell Gwen was different right from the start. Something about the light in her eyes told me that she had ways of seeing that were . . . well, you know, different from normal people.

I liked that about her. Of course. I like different.

It reminds me of me.

But Amity? Well.

Amity doesn't care much about different. Amity doesn't care much about anything, does she? Amity just wants what she wants.

Twenty-eight days. Barely a month. That's how long they lasted, the Halls, at Amity.

Exactly the same as us.

—Connor

PART I

ARRIVAL

TEN YEARS EARLIER
DAY 1

CONNOR

IT WAS HOT ON THE DAY WE MOVED IN, brutally hot, in that way that makes you feel almost crazy, sweat dripping into your eyes so bad you're practically blind. When we first pulled up in the van, Amity glimmered so you could almost see the ripples of heat with your own eyes, like a mirage plunked down far outside a tiny New England town. It wasn't a day for heavy lifting; only a crazy person would have tried moving all on their own, in that kind of weather.

But no one ever said that Dad wasn't completely insane.

Even being so close to the water, the sun was near unbearable. When Jules whined, Dad fixed her with one of his looks. Dad was never known for his patience. Not like me. I can be very patient. When it's useful, I mean.

Normal people would have hired movers, professional guys, to get the job done. But Dad said, "Why would I pay hard-earned money when we've got four pairs of hands among us?"

Yeah. *Four pairs,* so at least he wasn't expecting Abel to do much lugging.

Abel was only six, but you kind of never knew with Dad.

I just hoped that even then, even little, my brother knew he was getting a pass. Dad wasn't much for passes. This was definitely your onetime-deal kind of thing.

There were no onetime-deal passes for Jules, or for me. Seventeen, I wasn't an athlete at all—team sports rubbed me the wrong way—but I was strong enough.

Strong enough for some stuff.

So there we were on moving day. Jules whined, Dad glared, Abel mewled, and Mom worried. And I hitched my shorts up, and wrangled a box marked FRAGILE in six different places. It made a clinking sound as I hiked down the drive and past Mom, who made a face at the tinkle of shattered glass.

Our first day in Amity, and things were already all falling apart.

MOM HAD BOUGHT THIS SIGN, I REMEMBER.

Seriously, it was the stupidest thing. Like so stupid, I mean, that you almost had to feel all sorry for her for even having it. For, like, going into a store, and seeing it, and thinking, *Yes, I want* that, *I should have* that *thing*, and then paying real, actual money to own it. I can't even tell you. I didn't even know where you could find something stupid like that, a sign for a house.

AMITY, it said: this fake etching on a cheap, shiny, little fake-wooden plaque. She must've had it made up special, which made the whole thing even dumber. I didn't know anyone whose house had a name. It was the kind of thing you'd see in a movie, like if someone were rich or whatever. But no rich person would buy something tacky like this.

We weren't rich. I mean, we weren't poor. Which I guess meant we were in the middle. Probably from the outside it looked like we were doing better than we really were. That was Dad's thing—making sure we looked like we were doing better, doing well. God only knew what his sketchy "business" deals were. He had to sell off the Ford dealership downstate real quick, and I knew some neighbors had their own theories about his work. None of them were all that flattering.

But even with Concord being a little speck on the map, the kind of small town even small-town people are bored by, it was pretty, sort of. Like respectable. The kind of place you could maybe put down roots, not the kind of place you rushed to, all cowering in the dead of night, your stuff piled sky-high in the back of a pickup, no forwarding address left behind.

Concord was a respectable town, one of the oldest in the country. I guess Dad picked it thinking some respectability might rub off on us.

Also, the house came cheap. I didn't know why at the time.

I didn't care much about things like what a house cost, but I had to admit that Amity was nice. It was pretty big. Much bigger than our old place. In Amity, my bedroom was connected to Jules's by a bathroom we had all to ourselves. That bathroom felt like a real, big-time luxury after sharing just a single john with Mom and Dad for so long. It had one of those ancient bathtubs with the heavy iron claw feet that looked about a hundred years old. Jules thought it was cute but I thought you had to wonder how many people had soaked their bones in a tub that old, and where those people were now. And Abel's room was way down the hall, so for the first time in forever Jules and I wouldn't be woken by him at the unholy crack of *what-the-sweet-living-Jesus* every day.

On the third floor, there was a room I hoped for a second would be a den or something, like for me and Jules to hang out in, especially since Dad wasn't one for sharing the old remote in the family room. It would've been nice to have a space of our own just to, you know, *be* in. But Mom said it was going to be her "sewing room," like we were living in a fifties sitcom, so that was that. Never mind that I couldn't remember the last time I saw her sew. Jules was always trying to get me to go easier on the old lady anyway.

Hanging that sign from the mailbox was Mom's first and last sitcom moment at Amity, it turned out. And she never did spend any real time in that sewing room.

I remember moving day, and her linking the plaque through some hooks that'd been in the mailbox before we even arrived—I thought it was funny or just dumb luck or something that the hooks were already in, like they'd been waiting for us. Dumb luck didn't come easy to Mom. Or me, or Jules, now that you mention it. Any of us. But Mom smiled as she slipped the cruddy little sign in place, and then stepped back, holding a hand flat over her gray-green eyes to shield them from the sun.

Amity. It was ours now.

Mom had another little smile as the sign swung in the slow afternoon breeze. Even though we were in the real dog days of summer, there was a breeze coming off the Concord River.

She caught me looking at her. "What do you think, Con?" Her voice turned up at the end. Mom's voice always turned up at the end. It made everything she said into a question, even stuff that wasn't supposed to be, which says everything you need to know about Mom.

I shrugged, ignoring the little twitch of disappointment on her face as she tucked a stray, gray-streaked curl behind her ear.

I could have said a lot of things then: How we weren't the kind of people who named their houses—even if *Amity* did seem like the exact right name for this place. How you couldn't, like, change the future, alter your destiny just through the power of positive thinking, you know? How hoping didn't make things happen. *Couldn't* make things happen.

How, really, it would take much more than just moving upstate to turn things around for the Webb family.

But I didn't say any of those things out loud, and that slow grin stayed at the corners of her mouth.

"It's cute!"

Jules came up behind me. She beamed at Mom, her cheeks all pink and shiny from the humidity. She fixed me with a crooked frown, and shoved an elbow into my ribs. She flashed "thumbs-up" to Mom. "I love it!"

I cocked an eyebrow. "You *love* it?" Too far, even for Jules. It was a *sign*, you know? I mean, a *really stupid* sign, honestly. "Stupid." I actually said that part out loud, though I didn't mean to.

"I *love* it. *Love.*" Jules poked me again. "Don't be a jerk. That's Dad's job."

Fair enough.

Jules was the only person who could make me see reason. Just a weird twin thing, I guess. She was the one who kept me grounded . . . when I *was* grounded, I mean.

"Speaking of . . . ," I said.

Jules wound her mass of bright copper curls into a knot at the base of her neck, patting it in place, and fanned her face with her hand. I thought then how funny it was that we were actually twins, seeing as how we looked and acted like two people who hadn't even grown up on the same planet, much less in the same family. Jules's personality was like her hair: thick and wild, impossible to ignore.

Mine was just, you know, brown. Wavyish brown.

"He's down at the boathouse with Abel," she said, gesturing. "That little shed at the base of the dock. Apparently, someone left some tools and stuff in there."

"He's pissed that stuff was left behind. Or—wait, he's pissed that nothing good was left behind."

"Bingo." She frowned.

There aren't too many things that get to me, but Jules's frown does. That twin thing, maybe? Whatever it was, Jules's smile was just about the only "real" thing I knew. So I preferred when she was happy.

I reached out and pinched the tip of her nose, which I knew she hated, but which always made her laugh anyway. She snorted back a giggle, like always, and ducked, swatting my hand. Then she sighed, folding her arms across her chest. "It's so weird."

I followed her gaze. "What? The way the house is, like, sideways?"

It *was* weird, kind of. Whoever designed Amity was trying to make the most of the land they had to work with, I guess; since the lot was deeper than it was wide, the house sat perpendicular from the road. So it was the side that looked out at you as you pulled up the drive, not the front.

And it *did* look out at you, eerily. That's what Jules meant. That *Amity* sensed you.

That sewing room on the third floor had these little half-moon windows, like blank bookends opening out onto the road. They turned in toward each other, winking in the sun. They almost looked like—

"They look like *eyes*," Jules said. Her voice was low and

breathy now. "Beady little eyes, just staring down at you." She shivered.

"Yeah."

She turned to me. "Does it give *you* the creeps?"

I shrugged. "It's a house," I said, like that explained anything.

It didn't, of course. Maybe Amity *was* just a house, but there was still that feeling that it was . . . *aware*, that it was breathing somehow. Seeing you.

But it still didn't give me the creeps.

"Right, of course," Jules said. "Nothing creeps *you* out."

"It's a *house*," I said again, which still wasn't really an explanation.

We heard a smash, followed by Mom's usual desperate squeak. Something about the wind on the river made the sounds hazy, but Dad was for sure on another tear. Jules widened those sea-green eyes of hers and ran off. The only thing to do when Dad went off was to get gone.

I paused for a minute before following, but I didn't stop to wonder whether Amity was watching me go.

It was only a *house*, after all.

And nothing creeped *me* out. Never did.

Never does.

MOM CRIED DURING DINNER, so Abel did, too. I swear, the slightest thing can set him off.

I can relate.

You'd think move-in day would be all hopeful, maybe? The promise of new beginnings, or whatever. And maybe for some people—for some families, I mean—it is. Or it can be.

I wouldn't know.

All I could see were stacks of unpacked boxes, the monster-sized clumps of dust in the corners, the chip in Abel's favorite drinking glass, which didn't survive the ride up intact.

Did any of us?

We ate greasy pizza straight out of the box, sitting Indian-style on the dining room floor. A dusty chandelier that was still hanging when we showed up swayed, threatening, with any little breeze. Good thing the air was mostly as thick as the mood. It was quiet in that live-wire way. I could hear myself chewing from inside my head, and the clench in my throat when I swallowed. Abel mouth-breathed while he gnawed at his own food.

Then the telephone rang. It was a scratched-up, black rotary thing that had to be as old as the Concord River. Mom's eyes flew open soon as that bell sounded, and she flashed a glance at Dad, all panicked. I didn't think they were so free with their forwarding number when we hit the road, so the call probably wasn't coming from the local Welcome Wagon.

"It's loud," Abel said through a mouthful of cheese. It was. The ring of the telephone cut into me, sending little vibrations buzzing in the floorboards. "Should someone—" He snapped his mouth shut when Mom put a hand on the back of his neck.

Dad cleared his throat, hacking into his closed fist. We all knew that closed fist well enough, which was why Mom cut Abel off when she did.

"Annie, answer the phone," Dad said.

Jules—Julianne, that is (she went from *Annie* to *Jules* with everyone but Dad by our fifth birthday)—nodded and jumped up. She scampered over to the doorway to the kitchen, grabbing at the receiver and cutting the phone off mid-ring. "Hello."

I waited, itching to see who was on the line. The floorboards prickled at the backs of my thighs.

"*Hello?*"

She frowned. She held the receiver at arm's length so the cord popped and snaked like something alive. From across the room, I swore I could just make it out: the low hum of static, cracking and sparking like a whisper. Like Amity was calling out to us, almost, from those angry, thrumming floorboards.

Jules hung the phone up abruptly. She came back into the dining room, but stayed leaning against the far wall, like she didn't want to get that close to Dad right then.

"There was no one there," she reported, like we hadn't all just heard that for ourselves. "Maybe it was a wrong number."

Dad grumbled something, stood up, and lumbered to the phone, grabbing the receiver in his hammy, callused fist. Grunting, he stared at it like he could just sort of . . . *will* it to tell us our fortune, to tell us how things would be here at Amity.

I thought, *I could tell you.*

And I didn't know what I meant by that.

But I still knew it was the truth.

"YOU BE CAREFUL WHAT YOU TELL PEOPLE when you answer the phone."

Dad glowered at Jules—*past* her, really. Vacant. His eyes were flat.

"She's always careful," I said. We were all careful, in our own way. You learned to be, right from the start. Thanks to Dad.

"I'm—I will," Jules stammered. "I will." She shot me a look, asking me not to make things worse. That was always Jules's part to play: damage control. I rolled my eyes at her, small enough that no one but she could see, and tore my chewed-up crust in half.

Then came the crying. That was always Mom's part to play.

Her tears were sudden, like a faucet coming on out of nowhere. It reminded me of the sound Butch, our old pit bull mix, made years ago when I ran over his tail with the front tire of my mountain bike.

That was an accident, of course.

Old Butch was long gone, and Dad never let us replace him no matter how much Jules begged. That might've been my fault. But that yelp Butch made when he was hurt, it wasn't a sound you could just forget.

It grated, made my skin feel too tight. Kind of like Mom's crying was doing now.

Jules scrambled over to squeeze Mom's shoulder. "It's okay," she said. "New places are hard. Change is hard. It'll be fine.

"It just takes time."

She sounded so sure. Maybe she just wanted to shut Mom up before the waterworks could get worse. As it was, Mom's slobbering made Abel screw up his face even tighter, balling his fists all up at his sides.

Dad sighed, then pulled the phone cord out of the wall, leaving it to dangle like a loose thread, or a noose.

A noose?

Yeah, I thought, watching the loop of the cord sway. *A noose.*

"It'll be fine. It'll be *good.*" Jules really meant it, I could tell.

Maybe she felt what I did: that low hum from underneath, lulling me. I couldn't explain it—it would've probably sounded crazy if I tried—but Amity felt sturdy beneath me, like she had . . . *good bones.*

Amity felt safe to me, right from the start.

Jules wasn't worried about Amity.

Neither was I.

I WAS WASHING UP, sawing a toothbrush back and forth in my mouth while the water in the thousand-year-old faucet splashed back up onto my face like rain on a windshield.

I was actually feeling a little hypnotized, watching the trickle from the faucet seep down the opening of the drain. There was a smell coming from the drain while I brushed, scrubbing until my gums felt raw and bloody. It was like wet leaves gone kind of rotten. I spat, and the foamy dribble was cloudy pink. I shut the water off, twisting the taps tight enough to wrench my wrists. The faucet clanged off with a rattle.

That was when I heard it. The telephone.

It rang out, just like during dinner, all sharp and accusing. I went into the hallway to see if anyone was going to answer it, but the doors to all the other bedrooms were closed. I could hear the noises of everyone getting settled in for the night. The phone rang one more time, and I stood there, stock-still in the hallway, curling my bare toes against the wide, rough floor planks.

The phone cut off mid-ring.

I heard a doorknob rattle and realized that Jules had come into our bathroom from her bedroom. "You don't knock?"

"Sorry," she started. Then she saw the bloody, phlegmy mess in the sink. "Gross, Connor. If we're going to be sharing the bathroom, we need to set up some ground rules."

"Like knocking."

She sighed, the little breath sending the shorter curls dangling over her eyes bouncing. "Fine. Whatever."

I moved into the bathroom and shoved her aside, maybe a little harder than I really needed to, but not hard enough to hurt her or anything. I wasn't that way with Jules. "I'll rinse it. God."

I twisted the taps back on and splashed the spurt of water around, watching as the gobs of foam and flecks of pink washed away. When everything was clean enough again, I looked at Jules. "So who do you think keeps calling?"

Jules's eyebrows came together. "What, at dinner?"

"And just now." It was still kind of echoing in my eardrums.

She tilted her head. "What are you talking about?"

"You were in your room. You didn't hear it?" In old houses, sometimes sound carried weird and stuff. "It rang, again. Just now."

Jules put her hands on her hips. Her eyes were that mossy green they sometimes turned when she was really, kind of . . . *feeling*.

"Connor," she said. She sounded really tired and fed up. "Just don't. Come on. Dad unplugged the phone. You *saw* him do it. And look." She pointed to the end of the hallway where Mom and Dad's doorway loomed. "He was serious about not wanting any calls out here. No one he wants to hear from. Shocker."

I followed her arm, and blinked. I'd been standing here, just seconds ago, literally, all by myself in the hallway. And there was nothing—not one single thing—to see when I'd looked around. But there it was, right where Jules was pointing, coiled like a snake.

The phone cord. The *only* phone cord, from the only phone in the house. Still black, and twisted like a vine.

Or *vines*, I thought, like more than one. Because sometime between after dinner and now, Dad had hacked the cord into pieces and dropped them in a pile outside of his bedroom door, a wiry little nest of tiny black tentacles.

That echoing, thrumming sound was back, humming against the soles of my feet, and when I looked at the pile of phone cord again, it felt like the door behind it buckled. For a second, I thought that if I wanted to, I could have passed straight through the door myself.

"Keep it together, big brother." She clapped me on the back. "You didn't hear the phone ring again. There *is* no phone to ring again. And I . . . well. Keep it together." She said it softer the second time.

I heard the bathroom door slam behind her, but didn't turn. I couldn't look away from the shredded phone cord. It didn't matter what I could see with my own two eyes, or what Jules needed from me, how she needed me to be. I knew what I'd heard.

There is *no phone to ring,* Jules said.

But it *did.* It rang, and I heard it.

And I was the only one who did.

I didn't know what that meant—to be the person who heard the phone ringing. But I thought it meant *something.*

I smiled, and went back to my room.

I WAS READING—SOME ANCIENT, BATTERED TRUE-CRIME CRAP from a used bookstore when Jules popped her head into my bedroom. I couldn't even say what the book was, but that didn't matter. They're all the same anyway. I'd just got to the good stuff. Some not-so-great things were happening to a cute brunette with the bad luck to end up in a stalled elevator with a deranged ex-con. (Cute women should avoid situations like stalled elevator cars, but where would the fun be in that?) I'm not much of a reader or anything, but I was pretty well into things when Jules peeked in, so her quiet "Hey" sent me straight up in bed, like I'd been goosed.

"Hey." I was annoyed but pushing it down, putting the book facedown next to me to keep my place. If Jules was still thinking about the thing with the phone, she was pretending she wasn't. That things were all normal, which I preferred.

"You found the books?" She nodded at my cracked paperback. "I went through so many boxes . . . decided it was a lost cause for tonight. I'm too fried to hunt anymore."

"I just got lucky, I guess. Kept it in my bag, close all day."

"Smart," Jules said. "I have no idea where any of my stuff is. It took me an hour just to find this sweatshirt." She fingered the well-worn cotton, then shivered, rubbing her arms hard. "This house is freezing. Aren't you freezing?"

"Jules, it's August."

It wasn't really an answer to her question. Truth was, it *was* cold in the house. Strange, given how soupy and thick the heat felt just hours ago. But it didn't bother me too much. Neither did the cold itself. We'd packed up sleeping bags, separate from all of the boxes and other crap—Mom's idea, and a good one, even if she did pose it all uncertain and questioning, like always. So I was stuffed in mine right now, stretched out on a bare mattress on the floor. The chill couldn't reach me in here.

I felt safe.

"I *know* what month it is, Connor." Jules made a face. "It's still freezing in here." She shivered again, more dramatic this time, and let her eyes go to the window behind me. "It must be because we're right on the river."

Her expression went dark. "This window is filthy." She tapped at the smudged glass, then jerked back, like it was hot.

"Feel free to clean it," I snapped. All at once, I didn't want her touching that windowpane, didn't want her putting her hands on Amity again. "Tomorrow. I'm going to sleep."

She rolled her eyes. "Calm down. Sleep. No one's stopping you." But she twisted her mouth into another little grimace as she leaned, kind of tentative, toward the window again, so close she could have breathed rings onto the glass herself, if she wanted to.

She *didn't* want to. She pulled back again.

"Tomorrow I'm going to hang shades," she said quick, definitive. Then, like an afterthought, "Sleep tight." She turned and left the room.

"You too," I called, after a beat.

But she was moving away, through the bathroom door, maybe to wash her hands again after griming them up on the window. So she didn't hear me. I might as well have been talking to myself.

I might as well have been talking to Amity.

I WOKE UP DISORIENTED, thrashing like an animal inside my sleeping bag. I was slick, bathed in sweat.

It was what waking up in your own burial shroud would feel like, I thought. I wasn't sure where that idea came from, but it was vivid to me right then. I woke up feeling like I'd just come back from death.

Honestly, I've always felt like a little part of me's been dead since the day I was born.

So this waking up thing, it was almost like coming back, like a jagged moment that reached out and pinched me through the dark, heavy hood I hide under most of the time.

Strange.

Missing that hood, I took a quick scan of what was real, right then and there: I'd been dreaming. Slowly, I wriggled one arm out of the bag, fiddling with the zipper until the bedroll unfurled, letting the cool air blast my legs.

I was still only semi-awake. But dimly, in some miles-away corner of my brain, I could hear a steady clap, a banging, that reminded me of firecrackers, or that old cap gun I used to aim at the neighbors' cat. Back when I was younger, downstate.

(Just about the only fun times I could remember from downstate.)

But, wait.

Forget firecrackers, the cat. Forget downstate.

Like the burial shroud, it was one of those thoughts that bubbled up from nowhere. It was a clear image, solid and sturdy.

A shotgun.

I saw it: a cold, heavy shotgun, twin barrels trained . . .

Where?

I couldn't say. But not on me, I didn't think. So, *where*, then? Steel barrels, like close-set eyes, bearing down . . .

And then the image was gone. Vaporized. Along with that feeling of thick, bleak . . . *something*, I couldn't even say what.

It was gone.

I exhaled. Piece by piece, the room came back into focus. That's when I realized:

The window over my bed was open.

Not too much. Not, like, *wide* open or anything. Just cracked an inch or two. But, yeah: open. And Jules had made that whole big thing about the window, and how dirty it was, and getting all creeped out by it. And she went on about how cold it was in the room earlier, too. And what was especially nuts about it all was how it *was* so cold, even in August. Even with that dirty, creepy window closed.

But it was open now. No doubt about it.

And that damned clapping noise from outside banged out a crazy Morse code.

The boathouse, I decided. *Dad must've forgotten to fasten the door latch when he finished down there.*

I sat up, kneeling at the window, fingertips braced against the sill, and watched, almost hypnotized, as the boathouse door swung open and closed, open and closed, open and closed, again, and again, and again.

Open and closed.

Open and closed.

Open and closed.

Again.

And again.

And again.

The wind howled, sharp. I moved to pull the window shut, jimmying it a little to get it sitting tight against the sill. The moonlight, higher now, bounced against the pane, and I saw what Jules meant about the window being dirty. It *was* dirty—really *filthy*, like she'd said, smeared and cloudy and maybe even crusted over with something yellowish and chipping. But now that I was standing just a few inches in front of it, I could see that it wasn't *just* streaky. The smears and clouds caked onto the glass made a raised pattern, like bathed in spotlight, shining and calling to me.

A handprint.

On the window, spiraling out into five perfect points, a ghostly splotch hollowed away where the palm would be, was a handprint.

It looked about the size of my own hand, I thought. Like it could have almost been my own handprint, even though, obviously, it wasn't. It was pretty much the exact same size as my hand.

So I stretched my hand out, covering the print, and pressed down, hard, against the window.

The room fell away.

Amity pulled back a corner of the curtain.

THE FACE IN THE WINDOW'S REFLECTION WASN'T MINE.
Honestly, the face in the window wasn't even really a face, given its state. Human. Or whatever it was, once. *When*ever it was.

It would have been direct at eye level, peering right at me, but peering wasn't an option. Because its eye sockets—muddy and shining with riverbank muck—were hollow, running with flecks of dirt and thick, yellow pus. Something twitched and wiggled from the goop and I watched as a fat centipede slithered out and slipped down one cheek.

Its mouth—the place where a mouth would have been on a person, I mean—hinged open, slow and creaky. A fuzzy, decaying tongue, black with mold, flapped uselessly while those scooped-out, gunked-up eye sockets gazed, blank and intense.

It was trying to *talk* to me.

I smiled.

I touched my forehead to the glass.

There was another flash, from inside or outside of my own head, I couldn't really say. The face, the *thing*, dropped away, and it was just my own hand against that caked-on handprint again, and another shuddering bang. In the distance, the flick of a tail disappeared through the swinging boathouse door. It looked bigger than any backcountry animal I could think of.

(And I was pretty familiar with backcountry animals, what with all of my hobbies and pastimes and stuff.)

Then the door clapped shut for what sounded like—what *felt* like—good. One big last gust of wind, and then, in a blink, I couldn't be sure I'd seen anything at all. No matter how much I wanted to believe.

I glanced at the clock on my nightstand.

It was 3:14 a.m.

NOW

DAY 1

GWEN

THE SKY CHURNED VIOLENT SWIRLS of stormy violet steel on the day we came to Amity, thunder clapping so forcefully that the house herself repeatedly sighed in protest as we went about adopting our new home. Again and again I heard them: creaky, grudging bows, buckles, growing pains from a structure we'd been told was some two hundred years old, and then some.

From the way the house hugged her gentle slope of land, looking at once weathered, and yet still somehow eternal, two hundred years seemed a reasonable estimate of Amity's age. At least.

Our rented truck veered uneasily around the bend of the lonely country drive. No neighbors here, not for several miles; that was something new, something else to which we'd have to adjust. Only as we turned the corner did I see how odd Amity's perch actually was. The house was oriented perpendicularly to the road. Probably, Amity had been built before the road itself even existed. So it was the side of the house that came into view as we approached. The side, with a winking set of third-level windows that peered out, coldly curious, rather than anything as expected—or as welcoming—as a front door.

Amity gave you her back as you approached her. That was

the first thing I noticed about her. Her back, and her unsettling seat overlooking the Concord River. And of course, the hammering, relentless storm that I might have called *portentous*, if I wasn't discouraged by my parents from using such words.

The rain pounded down in sheets, whipping the churning river into frantic egg-white caps. This type of storm, the air syrup-thick and the sky abstract and hostile, was palpable to me. It felt like something I could grasp, could access somehow. Could maybe even harness.

But those thoughts were also discouraged, as a rule.

On our third trip to the truck, Luke pinched me as I climbed into the dank, echoing cargo bed. The rain pinging against the roof recalled for me hailstones—or pebbles, even, bouncing overhead.

I leaned against a cardboard box, its corner pressing into the meat of my thigh, and looked at Luke. His sand-colored curls were plastered against his forehead, and droplets of rain clung to his eyelashes. His T-shirt was one shade darker now, a deep forest green instead of sage, soaked through from the storm, and his jeans dripped a widening puddle on the floor around his feet.

"Ow." I rubbed at the spot on my forearm where he'd pinched me, and pouted even though it didn't hurt, and even though he knew that.

"Merry sunshine." He ran his fingers through his wet hair and shook his head like Murray, our spaniel mix, would. "Lighten up, Gwen. You're acting like it's a funeral or something."

Or something. Because it was a move, not a funeral. Not

at all. Because I wasn't dead, was I? Dead girls weren't fussed about things like weather. Or much else.

"I'm fine."

"You are a bad liar, little sis."

I couldn't hide anything from Luke. We were separated by barely a year, but we were connected, like I imagined conjoined twins were, and he could be fiercely protective, playing "big brother" despite the negligible difference in our ages.

I gnawed at my lower lip, tasting that murky tang particular to rainwater. "I'm just . . . It's embarrassing. That we had to move." *Because of me.*

Luke reached forward. Thinking he meant to hug me, I leaned toward him, only to realize he was brushing a stray leaf from my shoulder. I shivered, feeling foolish.

"There are worse things than being embarrassed," he pointed out.

"True."

Though I couldn't think of any specific examples just then, I had the very clear idea that there would be time enough for those. It was a sense that poured over me, sodden as the weather.

"Gwen," Luke said, and this time he laid a palm flat against my shoulder, firmly enough that gooseflesh pebbled my skin against the wet, cold fabric of my tank top. "You don't want Mom and Dad to worry."

Meaning: *Shake it off.* Allow this dreary foreboding to slide down my shoulders as easily as rainfall for our parents' sake. (And, therefore, my own.)

I nodded, still shivering, and pushed off the box, knowing I'd find a bruise on the back of my pale thigh tomorrow.

"Come on," Luke said, gesturing at the remaining boxes. They framed him, penned him in like a cardboard maze. "Not much more to go."

He was right.

But then, as it turned out, so was I.

AUNT RO HAD SAID THAT SAGE WAS CLEANSING, her face sincere as she offered me an embroidered silk bag filled with several dry, dusty gray-green sprigs. This was on the day the movers arrived at our old house, my parents preoccupied enough that we didn't worry about them, about their distaste for our shared superstitions, our joint inclination toward magical thinking.

"It's important," Ro said, "to usher the good energy in. Proactively."

I had unzipped the bright, egg-yolk-colored bag and gently traced the tight twine knots with my fingertips, noting how thin and delicate the leaves felt. It was hard to imagine that anything so papery-fragile could wield power, but I knew well enough that my own expectations could clash against the actual, physical world that others experienced.

Aunt Ro was the same way. Our emotional connection was ambiguous by "normal" standards, but was taut, innate, almost a living organism. It was Ro and her superstitions I'd clung to feverishly at Laurel Valley, through the gauzy veil of morning meds, evening meds, through the inane monotony of fervent, confessional group therapy sessions.

Through the paralyzing insistence that my perception of the world was not, strictly speaking, wholly reliable. In fact, *I* was other, not those around me, those beyond Laurel Valley.

Aunt Ro, of course, was only *other* in that she seemed to understand me.

She was my mother's older sister, and they were very close, but I was the one who adored her. Ro was a force of nature, magnetic and colorful, bold as the bright yellow silk bag of sage. She was open, attuned to alternate frequencies in a way no one else I knew was. She was, maybe, the *only* person who understood me. Who didn't think—hadn't ever thought—that I needed Laurel Valley. She saw quirks, abnormalities, as blessings. She had plenty of her own.

Aunt Ro was different, and that made me feel better, more comfortable, more

(*safe*)

secure in being different, too.

So when she'd given me the sage, still faintly scented, like a sachet in its pouch, I'd nodded and assured her I'd find the best place to put it to use in our new home. "Start off on the right foot," she whispered, running a cool index finger across my cheek.

Now, as the rainstorm finally tapered off and dusk began to stain the late afternoon sky, I considered the ideal place to make my offering. Mom and Dad were gone, returning the moving van, and Luke had proclaimed himself "done for the day," disappearing into his new bedroom. Rather abruptly, to be honest. But since he'd left me alone (which was, for the moment, my preference), I could hardly take issue.

"It's best to get as close as possible to the foundation of the house," Ro had said. "Everything that grows comes from earth."

"The basement." It was as close to the earth as a house could get.

She pursed her lips. "The basement. You'll want to start from the ground up."

Then, of course, she had known nothing particular about Amity or her history. She was only offering what she thought was good advice. Even with everything that was to come, I could hardly bring myself to blame her. The sage had been meant to cleanse. With another house, another space, another plot of earth, it might have worked.

IT WAS AS DARK AS THE INSIDE OF A COFFIN at the top of the basement stairs. Outside, the rain had given way to a gusty, constant shriek of wind that sang through the walls of the house. Amity was large, but not preposterously so. Still, its Victorian farmhouse layout was filled with nooks and pockets, corners occasionally revealing odd-sized doors and skewed archways like Alice must have found through her looking glass. Luke was still upstairs in his bedroom, and the only sound I could make out was a persistent drip from the kitchen faucet.

Reflexively, I curled my fingers more firmly around the bag of sage. It was the wrong shade, that sunny, egg-yolk hue: too hopeful and insistent, so at odds with my mood.

All the more reason for the exercise, I thought.

I groped for a light switch and found one on my right; when I flicked it on, a bare bulb at the foot of the stairs glowed pale and ghostly, only a slight improvement from the pitch-black. I made my way downstairs, clutching the sage in one fist and a box of matches in the other. I tripped on the very last step and staggered, trying to regain my balance, telling myself that my growing unease came only from my stumble, and nothing more.

The footprint of Amity's basement was wide, as large and implausibly laid out as the house itself. Once my eyes adjusted to the dimness, the main space was something of a relic. A deflated couch rested along the wall supporting the staircase, a matted, moth-eaten pillow without a case flopped against one arm. The floor here was poured concrete. A round, braided rug in muddy earth tones lay before the couch, looking defeated and drab. An oily stain spiraled along its stitching. The air smelled of must and thick, clotting mold, rich and sulfurous. Involuntary tears sprang to my eyes.

Get out, I thought. *Leave now.* Nothing good in this world smelled the way that basement did. Nothing I wanted to know about.

But Ro had said to be proactive, to be positive. She was coming tomorrow, would know, as she always did, whether or not I had followed through.

Ro had said to get close to the earth.

I sighed, keeping my breath as shallow as possible. *Close to the earth.* There was still the issue of the concrete floor, which I thought might be a barrier to true cleansing. I could see, from the small column of light that swayed in time to the movement of the hanging bulb, that the basement shared the greater house's tricky perspective: a narrow passageway, basically a dugout, gave way on either side to small, stone-lined arches revealing grottoes floored with dirt and rubble.

Dirt and rubble. That sounded more promising.

I shuffled forward. I didn't allow myself to wonder why Amity should rest above a series of semi-excavated caves, since I couldn't imagine an explanation that would be remotely comforting. A few paces further and the mouth of one small grotto—a crawl space, really—yawned open, welcoming me eagerly, or threatening to swallow me whole.

THE FIRST TWO MATCHES THAT I TRIED sputtered and died out.

On my third attempt, the match struck with a rough scrape. When the flame licked blue-gold at my fingers, I held it to the bundle of herbs with only a fraction of hesitation.

The leaves caught quickly. As they smoked, I took them by the gathered stems, shaking my little voodoo bouquet along the perimeter of the room, taking care to deliberately scatter ash in each corner. This was what Ro had instructed, but even knowing I had her encouragement, even with a specific directive, I felt foolish there, in the shadows, waving burning kitchen spices along the dirt floor.

Ro had a friend from college who read tarot cards and tea leaves for a living; Ro claimed she'd predicted no fewer than five major disasters in recent history, but Mom's contempt for this woman bordered on fury. "Hokum," she called it. "New Age hoo-hah." As if *hoo-hah* were *cancer* or *famine* or *a violent crime, punishable by . . .*

Well, punishable. So it was those words whispering to me, through the dark, through my shame, through my irrational fears, my irrational thoughts. I pushed them down, tried to let them settle beneath the weight of that murky, pregnant air.

Rational thought was important, I knew. Imperative,

even. And rational thought told me, that truly, there was nothing I *needed* to cleanse the house against; that even if this house did have history, it couldn't be that much worse than my own. In fact, a change of location was expected to do me good.

Rational thought told me to trust my surroundings, not my addled mind.

Then with a *pop*, the lone lightbulb blew out, and the door at the top of the staircase swung shut.

I GASPED at the sudden eclipse, clinging to the dying glow of the burning sage. Again, the thought of a coffin came to me, lid closed as tight as a vault's. A clinking sounded. *Probably the furnace*, rational thought insisted. . . .

But then it was August.

The grottoes, Gwen.

Who had carved them? And why?

Those questions seemed much more pressing now. A mud-floor cellar was something I'd heard of, something one finds in the country. . . . But cave-like, rabbit-warren dugouts? Those were something else, something different. Or they could be, if one were prone to . . . *hokum* and *hoo-hah*. To hysteria.

If.

I breathed in, the moist air skating in the back of my throat. I wasn't too far from the staircase, *couldn't* be; once I found the banister, I'd be able to hobble upstairs, albeit blindly. The staircase *couldn't* be that far from where I stood, *rationally*, since I hadn't come very far past the main area of the basement. The sad, stained rug had to be just a few shuffles away from my reluctant feet. It *had* to be.

But it wasn't.

The sage had nearly burned out by now (though the idea that the basement was cleansed wasn't at all reassuring in

46

the bleak, tomb-like darkness). My breathing quickened along with my heartbeat, and as a familiar tingle I hadn't felt in many years came over my skin, I willed myself to regain control.

Slow, deep breath sounds filled the space, hammering out their own meaningless pattern.

I dropped the sage and placed my hand flat and firm against my chest, over my heart. It was still racing, still twisting and writhing to a manic inner rhythm. And I was gasping for air, almost hyperventilating. There was no question.

The slow, steady breaths I was hearing weren't my own.

I HEARD A FRANTIC DIGGING SOUND, desperate scrabbles against stone and loose, rocky soil. The breathing was louder now, and faster, too.

The matches, I thought. *You still have the matches.* I jammed a hand into my pocket and dug the matchbook out, tearing off a match and trying to steady my hands enough to light it. I dragged it against the strip of flint, pinching the cardboard ends of the book with my free hand, once, twice, three times, before it caught, a pinprick of illumination leaping up, like a tiny fairy sent to light my way.

(go away, crazy)

But I *wasn't* crazy. Not anymore.

I followed the small swath of light toward the breathing sounds, barely daring to breathe myself, fearful of what was down here in the cavernous black with me.

Or, perhaps, of what *wasn't*

(not real)

actually there.

(But I *wasn't* crazy, anymore!)

I wasn't.

I WASN'T.

"Murray!"

I swatted the dog lightly on his side. He felt solid, his fur warm and velvety. "You almost gave me a heart attack."

He didn't turn away from the corner he'd been worrying at, though, and the *scritch-scritch* of his nails against the wall pulsed and echoed. Now I heard a creak, and a click, and the door to the basement swung open, flooding the space with light, so that I could see exactly where I stood. . . .

Which was exactly at the base of the staircase, that sagging, sorry couch off to my right, cushions bowing out into a crooked frown. The light from the kitchen was bright and I squinted, raising a forearm protectively over my eyes.

"What the hell are you doing down there in the dark, Gwen?" It was Luke, his legs splayed apart in a superhero's stance, reduced to a grayscale outline against the relentless light from the kitchen.

"Murray came down here," I deflected, hoping he couldn't smell the burned sage, or wouldn't recognize the scent if he did. "He's"—I gestured to the dog's frantic scraping at the floor—"he's digging. I guess he found something." That tingle crept over me again, making my scalp clench and crawl—*go away, go away*—and I had to restrain myself

49

from bounding up the stairs at a tear. "The light blew out."

Luke's mouth twisted, an expression I couldn't quite read. "So come on up already."

I was glad to. I counted off between each footfall: *not crazy, one, not crazy, two, not crazy, three*, pacing myself "normally" as best I could. Murray didn't follow right away, but that didn't surprise me. Dogs are so attuned to household dynamics; I wasn't the alpha, and Murray'd always been Luke's dog anyway. Luke was the one who rescued him from the pound, a fact for which it seemed the dog would be forever grateful.

Luke slapped his thigh, and Murray trudged back up the stairs. The rattling of the basement door closing behind the dog settled my jangled nerves. Somewhat.

"You stink, dog," Luke said, smiling now. "What the hell did you get into down there?"

I wondered.

Putting aside, at least for the moment, the debate between rational and magical thinking, I only hoped the sage had done its work.

"SHE WAS SHOT IN THE HEAD!"

I sat bolt upright in bed, gasping, groping blindly at my chest, my face, my forehead. My heartbeat, like gunfire, threatened to shatter my rib cage with each desperate breath.

She was shot in the head.

Yes, that's what had happened. She'd been shot at close range through the back of her skull.

Of this, I was certain, though where the thought—the *knowledge*, I insisted, against all rationale—came from, I had no idea. My throat was dry, and my skin buzzed again, I noted dimly. Just who this *she* was, or where/when/why this horrific thing had happened to her . . . it was murky, a reflecting pool on an overcast day. But the absence of clear detail didn't lessen the truth of what I knew.

She was shot in the head.

Had I said those words aloud? I must not have; I hadn't woken anyone in the house. I switched on the bedside lamp and glanced at the small digital alarm clock tucked next to the lamp.

3:14 a.m.

It was a nightmare, I told myself, hoping that if I insisted it firmly enough, my mind would believe it to be true. *The first night in a new house. You're disoriented. It makes perfect sense.*

It *did*. Certainly, it made more sense than the dull throb at the base of my own skull, which I gingerly rubbed. What had caused it?

(She was shot in the head.)

But *I* hadn't been. Of course, *of course* I hadn't.

I swept my hair back from my face and slipped out from under the covers, toes curling up as my bare feet touched the wide, wooden beams of the floor. The floor was cold, unyielding, and after a moment I realized that the air in the bedroom was, too. Never mind the dog days of summer; something about butting up against the Concord riverbank meant that nightfall carried with it a bone-drenching chill.

I shuddered, and my skull gave a slight groan of protest.

Quickly, though, I realized that the noise I heard hadn't actually come from inside my own head. It was a low, insistent banging from the direction of the water that I could make out distantly. A beat that twisted, wrung my spine out like a wet washcloth.

(She was shot . . .)

The boathouse, I decided. *The door to the boathouse must not be locked.* But when I peered out the window of the bedroom, I couldn't see through the thick, low-hanging fog well enough to say whether or not I was right.

Of course you're right. What else could that banging be?

There wasn't anything else I could think of. Certainly nothing else that I *wanted* to think of.

And besides, there was Murray to consider. He was a gentle, good-natured mutt, but still protective. If there was something out there worth barking at, even a chipmunk, Murray would be barking. Barking was what dogs did.

Murray would *certainly* be barking.

He would.

Was it strange, then, that Murray *wasn't* barking? Surely there was at *least* a chipmunk out there. Concord was the country, after all.

You're just not used to the quiet, I told myself. *It's natural.*

It's okay. New places are hard.

Change is hard.

"It just takes time."

I whirled. That thought had come, impossibly, from *outside* of me. From beyond my own mind. I was certain of it.

Just as I was certain that *she'd* been shot in the head, whoever *she* was.

And, yes, Amity unnerved me from the moment we pulled up the pebbled drive; *yes*, those winking half-moon windows on the top floor were like eyes, tiny, lidless, peering *eyes* that burrowed into your core, but that was *silly.* That was *absurd.* To be unnerved, to be *afraid*, even, of a house.

A *house.*

To be afraid of Amity was insane.

It was only a *house*, built by human hands, inanimate, non-sentient. A structure, an object. Not a *being.*

I was perfectly safe in here, tucked up in the shadowed eaves, nestled in the belly of this

(*beast*)

house, Amity.

(*and the sage, you burned the sage*)

I'd burned the sage; did that make my current dread *more* reasonable, or less? I didn't know. I was confused, and also, half crazed from exhaustion.

I was being insane.

The window was open a crack, I realized, so I moved to nudge it closed. It jammed momentarily, then yielded with a groan, cracking down quickly enough to make me start at the unexpected clap, sharp as the snap of a wild animal's jaw. Through the window, I thought I saw the flip of a tail—bushy and streaked a rusty, coppery shade—gliding smoothly around the corner of the boathouse.

I didn't know of any animals with a tail like that.

You're being crazy, Gwen. The laugh I tried to force caught in my throat. *You are* going *crazy.*

Again.

This house is perfectly safe.

It was utterly absurd to think otherwise, I knew. Utterly ridiculous.

Utterly *insane.*

I PADDED TO THE BATHROOM, cautious not to wake the rest of the family, still insisting to myself how ridiculous it was to be so violently disturbed, so unsettled by Amity.

By a *house*.

Never mind the electric charge snaking down my spine, an insistent, greedy sensation I hadn't felt since . . .

(go away, crazy)

. . . well, it was better not to dwell on such things.

I slipped through the bathroom door, turned the light on, squinting against the sour, yellow-green glow it gave off. The pedestal sink stood solid and sturdy. I grasped either side of the basin in my trembling hands.

It was crazy to be so thrown, so unnerved by the house. It *was*.

But, despite that knowledge, I couldn't shake the sensation that somehow I wasn't alone in Amity.

Yes, my parents were sleeping just down the hall. And Luke's bedroom was right through the bathroom door. Murray was undoubtedly curled at the foot of Luke's bed, though what that dog would do in the face of an intruder, I couldn't imagine. He wasn't exactly trained in home security. That was never the point of a family pet, not for our family. I was the only Hall with a habit of feeling . . . insecure.

(*She was shot in the head.*)

The thought flickered again. I swallowed, and pushed it out of my mind.

My parents. Luke. Murray. They were here with me. I wasn't *alone*.

Of *course*, I wasn't alone in Amity.

But that knowledge offered little comfort. Whatever that feeling was, that *foreboding* . . . slithering over me like a high-voltage second skin . . .

Wherever it came from, it had nothing to do with an actual, physical presence in the house. It was more like a thundercloud, or the thick, static charge that the air takes on just before a summer storm. I couldn't explain it, not rationally. But I couldn't deny it, either. It was a voice, a whisper. But from the inside, from within my bones.

The mirror over the sink was ornate, but scratched in some places—it had been here when we arrived, and looked to be as old as the house—and it was covered in a fine layer of dust. I cleared a patch of the glass with the cuff of my pajama top, peering into the streaked surface at my reflection. Bruise-colored shadows tinged the hollows underneath my eyes.

The person in the mirror did not look particularly well.

The overhead light wavered, flickering gray for a moment,

(*old house, faulty wiring, go AWAY, crazy*)

and when it glowed yellow-green again, a wave of nausea overtook me, nearly knocking me off my feet.

In the reflection of the mirror, I wasn't alone.

THE GHOSTED GIRL PERCHED BEHIND ME IN THE MIRROR was young, about my age.

Her stare was blank, but forceful just the same. Her hair, reddish, was pulled back from her forehead severely, but even in the dusty mirror, I could see that it was dark and wet, stained and matted at her temples. A trickle of something—*blood?* Yes, I thought that it was blood—curved around the back of her neck, over one shoulder.

She reached up a hand to the mirror's edge. To me. When she drew her arm back to her side, five small rust-brown smudges appeared in the mirror, like a handprint. A handprint nearly the size of my own.

I screamed.

"GWEN."

I flinched, and opened my mouth to shriek again.

But before I could make a sound, a hand clapped over my mouth. I could smell the woodsy, spicy half-life of the soap that Luke always used. But even as I recognized my brother, a bright, blazing flash burst, scattering white confetti before my eyes.

I heard a shattering, snapping noise. When my vision cleared, the girl from the mirror was gone. It was just Luke and me, peering out. But now a jagged crack ran through the glass, a diagonal slash that rushed from the top of my brother's reflection's jugular to the bottom of my own.

I read his face easily. He wore the look that begged me not to fall apart, not to unravel, to just-please-God not shatter like the mirror had.

"It's a little creepy here," he admitted, putting a hand on my shoulder. "But come on, Gwen. You're stronger now. You have to be.

"If you lose it,

(again)

". . . If you lose it, I mean. You know how Mom and Dad will be."

I nodded. I knew. He took his hand from my mouth.

Now the only faces reflected in the mirror were mine and Luke's, which should have been comforting. But the angry fault line fractured our images so they sat ever-so-slightly askew in a way that was still unnerving. I tasted panic in my mouth like warm syrup, powerful and sweet.

"I saw an animal outside. It startled me." It was the only version of the truth I could use.

"We're in the country, Gwen," he said. "Get used to it." When his lips met in the mirror, they didn't line up.

"You two." Our mother's voice floated toward us, muffled and drowsy. "Did something break out there?"

Luke's eyes met mine in the mirror, high enough above the crack that his gaze was steady.

"I startled Gwen in the bathroom," he called. "And she dropped . . ." He fumbled. "The mirror broke. Sorry."

"As long as you're both okay." Mom's voice was low; she wouldn't remember this conversation come morning. Luckily.

"It's fine, we're fine." My voice warbled only slightly. "Good night."

"'Night." Her voice unwound, she slid backward into sleep again.

I turned to face Luke so I wouldn't have to look at, to think about the broken mirror. "It's fine," I said again, hoping I sounded more convincing. "I didn't mean to wake you."

Luke tugged at the hem of his T-shirt. "It's . . ." He sighed. "Whatever, Gwen. I'm glad it's nothing." He cast his eyes toward the crack in the mirror, then away again, lightning quick. "Just . . . I don't know, just splash some cold water on your face and get back to bed."

I told him I would. It was a fine idea.

Certainly better than any I had of my own.

ALONE AGAIN IN THE BATHROOM, I blinked and looked down at my fingertips, now as dusty as the mirror had been.

Cold water, Gwen. Splash some cold water on your face.

I reached out, twisted the sink's tap.

Water trickled out in a slow, stuttering sputter. I ran my hands palms up under the stream, rubbing them together until the grime and muck were rinsed away.

I shut my eyes.

The tap whistled and whispered, spouting a thin river into my cupped palms. I breathed in, out.

The faucet hiccupped.

My eyes flew open.

The faucet issued a quick, shallow belch, and the stream of cool water was staunched.

(what . . . ?)

That half-formed thought was all I had time for. The pipes leading into the wall clanged and trembled, sending another cough through the mouth of the faucet.

The tap began to run again.

This time, it was hot. Scalding. *Searing.*

And it was *red.*

I gasped and pulled my hands back to my chest, cupping

them against my body. I was so horrified by the grotesque torrents spurting out that my brain barely registered the pain.

The water. The *water*.

The water rushing from the tap was *red*.

Red, thick, and rusty.

The water spurting from the tap was red and rusty as an infected wound, and my hands, which had been submerged in it, had erupted in angry, swollen

(*gunshots?*)

blisters.

(*what when how?*)

I couldn't know. I couldn't say.

But I *did* know—again, still:

I wasn't alone. I *wasn't*. No matter what halfhearted reassurances I'd made to Luke, or to anyone else, I knew the truth.

I wasn't alone in Amity. Someone—some *thing*—was here with me. Lurking in the fault line of the mirror, maybe. Or maybe stirring now, eager to escape.

(*she was shot in the head*)

(*the head the head the HEAD*)

I clasped my blistered fists together and swallowed down a scream.

TEN YEARS EARLIER
DAY 2

CONNOR

THE HANDPRINT WAS GONE IN THE MORNING.

It was the first thing I did when I woke up—jumped out of bed and over to the window to check, I mean. But the window was wiped clean, or anyway: it was the same exact dirty that Jules had bitched about. It was streaky and dusty and strung up with cobwebs, yeah, but it was definitely not marked up with any handprint. Not anymore, if it ever was in the first place.

That made me pretty angry, if you want to know the truth. It felt a little like being lied to, which I don't like. That reflection—that dead-like, rotting thing in the window—That didn't get to me. I thought it wanted to talk to me, wanted to really get to know me, have a heart-to-heart or something, and I was okay with that. What bugged me was the not knowing for sure, the wondering. And the handprint being gone was confusing, mixed-up, and slippery the way things sometimes get in my head.

I threw on some clothes and wandered out into the hall-way, wondering if it was safe to head downstairs and scrounge up something to eat. Without the dealership, Dad wasn't work-ing regular hours, but I didn't think he'd be hanging around the house too much. He didn't really like spending time with any of us and the feeling was mutual. Except for Abel, maybe, who was still a little too young to know better, poor kid.

When I passed by Jules's room, her door was open. Quiet guitar-band music was playing: that airy, depressing girl stuff. I ducked inside. She was still in last night's pajama pants and that hoodie, all stretched out at the neck, sitting on her mattress with her knees pulled up to her chest, staring off at the door to our bathroom. Her room was a mirror image of mine; there weren't any special girlie touches up yet or anything. Just a lamp on her dresser. Its ruffled shade made the space look even sadder than if she'd left it completely bare.

"New places are hard," I said, parroting what she'd told Mom the night before. I was hoping for a laugh.

Jules shot me a dirty look, her eyes flashing. "You're funny."

She stood up and tightened the drawstring on her pajama pants, then reached to the scratched-up radio on the windowsill, turning it off. "Enough." The room felt extra-quiet, empty, without that *pity-me* strum playing in the background.

"What's your problem?" I asked, sounding more annoyed than I meant to. I was thinking of that *face*, bone-white with the oozing, gaping sockets where eyes should have been.

"I slept badly," she admitted. She tightened her hair elastic so her curls sprang up an inch higher at the back of her head. "I think . . . Well, I was cold. But also, the boathouse door. It kept banging and waking me up. It sounded like—"

"—like a shotgun," I said, jumping in, maybe a little too eager.

She looked at me, her mouth a tight line. "Yeah, exactly. But it didn't bother you." She said that last part angry.

"Well, you know." I shrugged. "Nothing ever bothers me, really. Nothing creeps me out." Another of her little sayings from yesterday back to haunt her.

She didn't think that was funny, either. And I *knew* why she was all annoyed. I could see why other people—why Jules—wouldn't make jokes about shotguns blasting in the dead of night. That wasn't normal, it wasn't the way regular people were supposed to think.

But the thing about it was, even if she didn't think it was funny . . .

I did.

IT WAS TRICKY WITH ME.

Whether I was feeling angry, whether I was having—or *not* having—normal-person reactions to things, I still reacted to *Jules*, you know. I didn't like to see her upset. So I told her I'd look at the door to the boathouse, see if there was something I could do to fix it. She seemed relieved, her ponytail relaxing, bobbing a few inches lower down her neck. That was good.

And if I maybe had some other secret kind of reason for wanting to get closer to the space? Like something maybe calling me from down there? Well . . . I kept that to myself right then.

And that was good, too.

MOM WOULDN'T HAVE WANTED ME TO TAKE THE CAR.
Wherever Dad was that morning, he didn't go there in our crappy four-door. But Mom wouldn't have been too keen on me taking it into town, on the off chance that Dad came home earlier than she expected and got it into his head to be bothered by the car being gone. Dad got bothered by things pretty easy.

I didn't care about Dad getting bothered—just another one of those things that was a problem for other people that just didn't get to me, right? And I didn't much care what Mom did or didn't want, either. So I didn't ask about the car. I just took it.

I knew where to find the keys. Dad was predictable. Back downstate, he kept them stuffed into his underwear drawer, tucked into his holey old shorts like a secret porn stash. I waited until after lunchtime when Mom, Abel, and Jules headed down to the river in their old, stretched-out bathing suits, Mom with a huge, billowing T-shirt over hers to cover everything up. Even with that circus tent brushing back and forth between her knees, you could still make out the yellow edges of a fading bruise peeking out like a frown. She tried, I guess, but there's only so much covering up you can really do.

Now, some people would disagree with my thinking here. (I do know a little bit about how other people think, what normal people usually say and do.) But if you ask me, in some ways Mom kind of deserved what she got. I mean, if she was going to go around trying to cover things up, how could she expect them to ever change, right? It was weak, that behavior, and if there's one thing I'm not, it's weak.

Still, that bruise—*all* the bruises—they made the edges of my vision go red, made my fingers clench around the firm metal of the car key. Maybe Mom was weak, but Dad was still evil, and even with my own . . . well, my own special way of seeing things . . . the way real life sometimes looked to me as flat as cardboard . . .

Well, I fucking hated Dad.

So when the ignition of the car turned over and the dashboard sparked to life, I gritted my teeth, hunkered down, and just barreled out of there.

Nobody could hear me down by the river anyway. I was pretty sure about that. That Concord River, she rushed.

THERE WAS ONLY ONE ROAD TO AMITY.

The house lay at the end of a long, twisting dead end. The only way past was by river, so in order to get to anything close to civilization, I drove back in the direction we came the day before, the dirt road already looking more uneven, more forgotten and overgrown than it did yesterday. This was real and true backcountry, but it felt almost jungle-like, with branches and bramble unwinding from gnarled tree trunks and clawing at the edge of the road, reaching for me. The air was humid and wet, stinking, all ripe like moss and overgrowth. And the way the leaves jittered on their branches, well . . . it sounded like they were whispering little messages to me.

As I squinted through the windshield, gripping the steering wheel so hard my knuckles were bone-white, I had a flash of that face again, that gaping, empty gaze from the night before, and I nodded, like I was answering those whispers myself. That shuddery feeling I kept getting around Amity swelled up in my stomach, light as air. Then it was gone, a soap bubble popped, and I nodded again, like I was reassuring the house and her . . . well, her *tentacles*, that's how those snarled, ragged branches felt right then—reassuring everything that was connected to Amity . . . that I'd be back.

And when the leaves rustled again, they told me they knew that I would be.

I thought then that Amity was already all mine. I didn't realize it was actually the other way around.

I FOLLOWED THE MAIN ROAD TOWARD TOWN, the roadside trees thinning out some, and the voices and the whispers quieting, too, the closer I got. But that soft hum, which felt so right, so welcoming, it was slowly getting replaced, like drowned out, I mean, with a popping loop of static. No matter how hard I listened, I couldn't make out whether the static was inside my head, or outside of it.

That happens to me sometimes. I don't worry too much about it.

The dirt road gave way to blacktop, although the pavement was patchy and maybe even tougher on the car's suspension than the dirt was. After a few more miles, a dotted yellow line, fading at some spots, appeared, telling me that people were here, that Real Life was up ahead. The static was suffocating now, like the knob on my mental radio had been turned all the way up.

There was a small convenience store kind of grocery up ahead, with a neon sign burned out black in three places. Two battered-looking cats padded around the parking lot, suspicious, hovering a couple paces away as I pulled in. As I made my way to the front door, they glared at me, wary. I kicked a leg out in their direction and they broke away.

I thought: *Weak.* All of them.

The door stuck when I pushed on it, and then the rubber tread on the floor gave a little coughing hiss when I leaned further. I watched the man behind the counter watching me, looking a little doubtful—challenging, even—while I shoved up against it. He gave a tiny jut of his chin when I stumbled in.

There was one other person in the store, a fat, bearded guy in a T-shirt pulled tight over his sagging beer gut. The top of his head was bald, with a semicircle of grayish fuzz hanging on for dear life, tracing a scraggly path from one temple to the other. The dull fluorescents overhead bounced off his bald patch. He flicked his eyes in my direction, then shifted a little. It wasn't like he had his back to me, completely, but there was an angle to the way he was standing. It wasn't friendly.

That was fine. I'm not always too friendly, either. It depends on the situation, you know? What the situation calls for.

Anyway. There was something I needed. For Jules. So I figured: *Who cares?* Just get in and get out. Get it done.

The man behind the counter plucked a toothpick from somewhere up alongside the register and popped it into his mouth, rolling it around on his tongue real energetic, keeping an eye on me the whole time. His friend still wasn't turned my way, really, but I could see his shoulders creep just a little bit higher toward his ears, his shirt catching on his belly and rolling up over itself.

"Do you know where the nearest hardware store is?" I asked, thumbs hitched into the pockets of my jeans. Through the angry fuzz of my headspace, I could hear how my voice sounded in the cold, stale fortress of the store, all flat and closed and not trying to make any good impression. I had a feeling that these guys, they wouldn't appreciate my tone,

73

the way it was so clear, how I felt so distant in my head, you know . . . but I didn't care.

"Or maybe you have something here," I went on. "I'm looking for a latch, you know, like for a shed. To keep the front doors closed. Even a set of chains and padlock would be good, if you had hooks for the chains. I've got a drill at home to get the hardware onto the doors."

Hell, maybe a padlock would be *better.* Maybe I could find a way to make that boathouse my own little hideout, or something. There had to be a way to make that happen, no matter what dear old Dad's plans were for the place.

When I wanted something, I usually found a way to make it happen. And now the static in my head was swarming, like a nest of wasps, buzzing, all eager, like really into the thought of making the boathouse my own. Right now that felt like a pretty terrific idea.

"I guess the wood might be pretty old, so I'm not sure how solid it is. But I'm pretty handy with a drill, so I think I could make do." I'd always been good with power tools, even before I started working part-time at the dealership, before I had any good reason to be handling drills.

The man behind the counter pulled the toothpick out of his mouth. He tossed it under the counter, where there might have been a trash can. He slapped one hand down on the Formica and leaned forward, the paunch of his midsection flopping over the edge of the counter.

"Yeah, I guess that wood's pretty old," he said, squinting until his eyes were mean, narrow little slits that were probably supposed to intimidate me. "Rotten. You're not going to get a drill through that crap."

I stepped a little bit closer. "You don't even—"

"—'Course I do. Amity, right?"

My face got hot and my throat felt tight. I must've given myself away. That didn't happen too often.

His friend, the one who'd been so determined not to look me in the eye, finally pivoted, swiveled on one scuffed-up work boot. "You can't come to a place small as Concord and expect people aren't going to notice."

Well, that was bad news for my dad, who had been hoping just that—that we'd come here and lie low for a while. That he'd outrun or just plain wait out his debts. But it made sense. A place as small as Concord? It was anonymous, yeah. But also—

"—you can't expect people aren't going to notice newcomers, not around here," the friend went on, rubbing a grease-stained thumb against his forefinger. "And you can't expect nothing to go into the wood at Amity. That place is rotted to the bone."

"To the bone," the man behind the counter agreed in a nasty singsong, sniggering. Wet little flecks of snot and dust floated in the air in front of his face, catching in those sour yellow overhead lights.

I nodded, those wasps in my brain flapping their wings real insistent now. "Are you . . . ?" *Are you trying to tell me something?*

The shop worker waved a hand. "Couldn't if we wanted to." As if he could hear what I was thinking out loud.

"Amity's different for everyone." His friend hitched up his pants with a squeaking little groan. Finally, he faced me direct, and nodded, sharp, right at me. "You just let us know how it goes for you." His tone said he meant just the opposite, that neither of them thought I'd be back to tell tales.

That I probably wouldn't get out, get away from the house again.

Are they right?

But more than that—did I care?

The wasps rushed forward, so determined it was all I could do to keep myself from moving forward with them, from grabbing both of these guys right around their pudgy necks and wringing until their faces were the same bright red that flashed in my eyes, on my tongue, under my fingertips.

I thought: *Never mind.*

I thought: Things would be just fine for me, with Amity. I wasn't like most people.

I wasn't the one who had anything to worry about.

"Thanks anyway," I said, short.

I decided to go straight back to Amity. I didn't bother checking out another hardware store, or any other place that might be nearby. Jules would just have to deal with the boat-house banging.

All those wings beating against my brain, they wanted me to get back home.

NOW

DAY 2

GWEN

BY THE LIGHT OF THE MORNING, things felt bright and airy again in a way that made me almost laugh to myself, sheepish, as I rubbed my eyes and propped myself up in bed. The sun streaming through my window was so vivid it nearly felt surreal, reluctant as I was to think about things in those terms.

The surreal was dangerous. Anything other than actual, real reality couldn't be trusted.

I couldn't trust my own mind.

But . . .

But what about my *eyes*?

I flexed my fingers gingerly beneath the covers. My left hand, the one that had been more doused, ached. The pain was dim, but solid enough, still present. The pain felt real.

But seeing was believing.

I drew in a nervous breath.

What are you afraid of, Gwen?

If the blisters that had formed last night were gone, then all was normal and safe again. Safe enough anyway. If my hands were intact, I could tell myself I'd been dreaming, seeing things last night, that I was hysterical, exhausted, out of sorts from the first night in a new house.

If my hands were unburned, unblemished, then all was

well. I'd only been having a moment of temporary . . .

Well, the expression is "temporary *insanity*," isn't it?

Yes. Insanity.

Everyone has those, Gwen. Everybody.

Everyone goes a bit crazy now and again.

If the blisters were still there—and they *felt* still there, oozing and prickling and protesting, angry and wet—

Well. If the blisters were still there, then this place, Amity—it wasn't safe.

If the blisters were still there, I had issues to worry about other than the question of my own insanity.

Everyone goes a bit crazy.

Now and again.

I slid my hands up, out from the covers, splaying them open before my eyes.

I WAS HUMMING AS I MADE MY WAY DOWNSTAIRS, memories of throbbing hands running off me like chalk lettering in the rain. I flexed the smooth, unmarred fingers of my left hand for good measure, cupping the cool, polished banister as I descended. It felt solid and reassuring.

The kitchen was thick with breakfast smells: coffee, bacon, anything swimming in a pool of butter. A pile of dishes in the sink confirmed that a meal had taken place sometime while I was still upstairs, cowering in bed. I tried to ignore the ripple of shame that rose at the thought.

I had just set a kettle of water on the stove when my mother wandered through the doorway, stretching her arms above her head.

"Good morning." She quickly crossed the room and kissed me on the cheek. "Did you sleep well?"

"I—"

(she was shot in the head)

"—I slept fine." I nodded.

"Me, too." She didn't seem to remember being woken. She inhaled again, deeper. "Must be the river air. I was out cold as soon as my head hit the pillow. I slept like the dead."

It was a figure of speech, of course. Still, she offered a nervous glance my way. I did my best to avoid taking a peek at the delicate blue road map of veins lacing my inner wrists. The blisters from last night were gone, but I had other scars.

Go away, go away. The refrain echoed like a pulse. *Sleeping like the dead is not the same as* being *dead.*

I knew that, of course.

A hollow pounding blared from the other side of the wall. "What's going on in the dining room?" I asked, deliberately (if not subtly) changing the subject. *Better not to talk about the sleep of the dead. Better not to think about it at all.*

"Home improvement." Luke appeared in the doorway, brandishing a hammer. "Mom wants shelves, Mom gets shelves."

"Mom wanted shelves before Ro gets here," Mom clarified. She looked at her watch. "Mom isn't convinced that's going to happen."

Luke's mouth twisted apologetically. "Mom has a healthy grasp of reality," he agreed. "Lunchtime feels really, really soon."

He winked at me, a tacit reminder that by daylight, all was swept clean. "Are you impressed by my manly-man skills?"

"Um," I said. "You were saying something about a healthy grasp of . . ." *Reality?* I tripped on the word.

"Correct," he replied, cheerfully spanning the broad space between the archway and the kitchen table with two smooth strides and placing the hammer down. "The walls here are kooky. I haven't been able to get a single nail in."

He pulled three bright orange mugs from an overhead cabinet as the teakettle began its pre-whistling hiccup of steam. Those mugs were a cheery, hopeful color, and it warmed me just to see them set there on the counter. A kettle on the burner, easy banter, and the still, calm air settling, feather-light, over our new house.

It was a cloudless morning, and I was a regular girl.

"There *is* something strange about the walls." Mom wrinkled her forehead. "Thick plaster? Heavy support beams? I wish I knew more about these things."

A shadow crossed the four-paned window overlooking the backyard, shading the room gray for a beat.

"I'll show you," Mom said.

Casting a questioning look back at Luke, I moved closer to the wall, hugging the curve that outlined where the dining room began. It was like running my hands across Braille. The plaster was speckled with pinpricks of varying sizes, a constellation of crumbly pockmarks.

I glanced to the floor. Nails were scattered, crooked and bent like beckoning fingers. "*None* of those would go into the wall?"

Mom shrugged. "Must be a stud there, or something." She knocked on the wall to demonstrate, but instead of the flat, expected reverberation, an echo called back.

It didn't *sound* like a stud.

It sounded like a chasm.

A cavern tucked away inside the walls of Amity. Those grottoes, that dank network of underground warrens from the basement came back to me, ringing an internal alarm. It didn't *sound* like a stud.

It sounded like a hideout.

But a hideout for *what*?

(*she was shot*)

My hands throbbed, sharp and insistent, the sudden, pulsing pain mimicking the flat echoes of Mom's raps against wall.

I tilted my chin down, trembling, and reluctantly I uncurled my right palm.

Hot yellow pus oozed from the raw, gaping mouth of a blister, a bloodless stigmata.

Gasping, I thrust my hands behind my back. Droplets of pus had pooled on the floor beneath me, and I willed my eyes away, willed my mother not to follow my gaze, not to see—or *not* see—my flesh, my fears, spilling forward.

(i slept like the dead)

(like the dead)

(the DEAD)

She knocked on the walls again, and again my hands twitched, prodded with imaginary pokers. "Who knows?" she said, sounding puzzled, not really concerned.

She reached for me, and though I shrank back, she grabbed my hand firmly in her own. I bit my tongue to avoid crying out, watching in horror as viscous fluid seeped between our interlaced fingers.

My mother, oblivious, squeezed my hand.

"Maybe we'll get that contractor back here. The one who did the inspection," she mused. "I'd love to get my hands on the original plans for the house."

Would you? Really?

She dropped my hand and stretched again, shaking out her shoulders like she'd suddenly gone completely boneless. Like she was made of rubber.

I waited a moment, then chanced another quick look at my hands. They were smooth again.

I decided it was just as well.

BETTER, FOR SO MANY REASONS, TO FOCUS ON
AUNT RO'S VISIT. She was coming for an overnight stay,
our first visitor at Amity. I would have been thrilled to see her
under any circumstances, never mind the grounding presence
she had on me, on my . . . unreliable nerves.

She was due to arrive around lunchtime. By eleven, I was
peering out the living room picture window every five minutes,
sipping rose hip tea from that deceptively cheerful orange mug,
hoping to see her key lime green convertible speed up our drive.
At 12:15 on the nose, I heard the welcome grind of her engine
shutting down out front, and dashed outside to greet her.

I was a few seconds behind Mom, and when I arrived
outside, the two were embracing, Hollywood-style, Ro's
arms firmly clasped around Mom's waist and twirling her a
few inches off the ground, despite her seemingly slight frame.
Ro was easy to underestimate, stronger than she looked. Her
silver-streaked hair was gathered in a braid that whipped back
and forth like a lightning bolt as she and Mom hugged and
giggled like little girls.

But when they broke apart, and Ro smoothed out the
puckers in her short, boxy sundress, I saw that her face looked
pinched, her color not its usual peachy flush. She was beautiful as always, but maybe not at her best.

84

I tried not to wonder why that might be. I was too excited to see her.

I threw my arms around her and squeezed, breathing in the musky lavender oil she always dabbed behind her ears. She grasped my shoulders, then slid her hands down my arms until her fingers covered my own. My palms prickled with sweat at the contact. She looked me in the eye.

The sage. Without words, she was asking me about the sage, and I dipped my chin in a quick nod. Her look of relief was imperceptible to anyone but me, I thought, which was probably as she intended.

My mother waved us toward the house. "You must be tired," Mom said, even though Ro's trip shouldn't have been too long. "Come inside and have something to drink."

"I was having rose hip tea," I said. "But there's also ginger, and some other stuff."

Ro's eyes lit up. "You read my mind, Gwen."

In Ro's case, I knew she meant it literally.

I DIDN'T HAVE TO READ RO'S MIND to know that she was taking in every last inch of Amity as we made our way through the house to the kitchen—and that she wasn't exactly liking what she was seeing. Her eyes skimmed over the wainscoting, the pocket doors, the crown moldings . . . but registered no joy, as my mother's had on moving day.

I couldn't completely ignore Ro's pallor, or the vague caution with which she regarded the

(*bones*)

beams and floorboards of the house. She was actually looking a little queasy, running her fingertips over the flocked floral patterns in the kitchen wallpaper, pressing into the raised texture like a foreign language, a Mayday appeal in Braille.

"Lemonade from scratch." Mom pulled a glass pitcher from the refrigerator and set it down on the table. She turned to pull three glasses from the cabinets, calling over her shoulder, "I was feeling very 'country.' Rural living suits me, surprise, surprise."

"Mmm," Ro murmured, her lips pressed into a line. "And Hal?"

Mom smiled, bemused. "You'll love this. He's been looking at secondhand boats—"

I felt a shock down my spine at the thought of the boathouse, that banging door reverberating like a death knell in the night.

Ro took a delicate sip of her lemonade and coughed. "Excuse me."

"Do you need sugar?" I asked. "Mom didn't put much in." I preferred things sugarcoated, saccharine to the point of cloying; not everyone shared my tastes, I knew. Still, I pushed the chipped ceramic bowl toward her.

Ro shook her head, patting at her chest as her coughs subsided. She looked at me, the gold flecks in her eyes catching the sunlight.

"Sugar just covers up the natural state of things," she said when her throat had cleared. "It takes away from what's most innate about a substance."

She traced a circle along the surface of the table and, beneath the tabletop, I felt the pressure of her foot tapping lightly at my own.

"Personally, I've never seen the point in that."

MOM HAD things to pick up at the market; she and Dad had come home from returning the van later than expected, and their grocery run to Concord was cut short. So I was tasked with giving Ro the grand tour of Amity mostly by default. But I was glad to do it anyway. Ro was livelier after the lemonade, but still not back to her usual self. It unnerved me.

"Should we go down to the river? It's cooler down there." I placed our empty glasses in the sink. Maybe the air would do her good. "Luke's been cleaning out the boathouse, I think."

I regretted the suggestion almost instantly, the insistent rattle of the boathouse door creeping again, stomping along my rib cage.

(*go away*)

As though she could hear the banging herself, Ro swallowed hard. That greenish tint rushed back into her cheeks.

"Maybe in a bit." She fingered at her handbag, a fringed, tribal-looking satchel bursting with clumps of folded-up paper and a plastic water bottle, half-empty, peeking out at an angle. She took a quick sip from the bottle and stuffed it back into the bag. "Why don't you show me the house?"

"Or I could always take you to your room," I offered quickly. "If you want to lie down? The house will still be here when you wake up."

Her eyes darted back and forth, like a small animal's. I thought back to that rust-colored flip of a tail I'd seen out my window last night. "Once I lie down, there's no telling when I'll be up again." She forced a short laugh, setting her bag on the table and patting it as if it were a household pet, some living, breathing familiar. "I'll leave this here. Why don't you show me around now, while I'm still at least semi-alert?"

In fact, she seemed acutely alert, almost like she was poised for an unexpected catastrophe.

I could relate.

"Sure," I said. "Let's go."

RO NOTICED the dining room wall right away. The hollow nail holes Luke made left the wall looking scarred. Her eyebrows twitched as we passed through the room, but she remained silent. She had been likewise still when I'd pointed out the door to the cellar on our way out of the kitchen. "Basement," I mumbled. "Boring."

Now, still eyeing the wall warily, Ro took a deep breath, the large, colorful beads of her necklace rolling against her freckled skin. "You burned the sage down there?"

I flushed, somehow ashamed, despite the suggestion—the order, really—having come from Ro herself in the first place. "In the corners," I confirmed. "Or as close to the corners as I could get. It's kind of a maze down there."

She rapped against the wall, just beneath one thick web of cracks left by Luke's hammer. Again, that round, hollow sound drifted toward us, the noise that had so puzzled my mother earlier.

"Yes," she said. "I see."

As we passed through the doorway toward the staircase, she ran a finger along the plaster archway. "Amity is an old house, Gwen."

I nodded. "A hundred years, at least. A thousand. A

million. I don't know, exactly. *Old.* It's been around—in one form or another—forever." The realtor must have told us as much; how else would I know?

"Forever. Yes, that sounds right."

One hand steady along the banister, Ro led the way upstairs. Her color was still off, uneasy, but her gait was sure, steady in the way I thought my aunt herself intrinsically was. Usually.

"The drive down was . . . Well. The roads around here are unreliable." Ro's words floated past her shoulder, toward me. "Did you all notice? Was it like that for you yesterday? When you came down?"

"What do you mean?"

"Lots of roadblocks and detours, the closer I got to Concord," she said. "Roads that didn't show up on any maps. The directions your mom gave were practically useless. I had to reorient myself every five miles or so. Very unsettling."

I shrugged, even though she was walking in front of me, and couldn't see it. "I didn't notice. Nobody mentioned anything like that." *Not to me.*

(*they wouldn't*)

"Right, and"— Ro seemed to be talking to herself as much as to me now—"I'm you're first visitor. And you just moved, don't know the area. You haven't met the neighbors yet, I'm assuming."

"Neighbors? We're out in the wilderness." The house sat alone on a hill, after all.

Ro's spine stiffened briefly, her fingers tensing against the banister. At the landing, she turned to me, her features arranged too cautiously to be entirely sincere. "Well, I hope you're not *too* isolated out here. It'd be nice if you could make some friends."

Nice. Because relationships were hard for me, connections were sometimes difficult, due to my

(*hysterical*)

sensitive nature, which so many of my peers found off-putting.

I stood beside Ro at the top of the staircase, taking in the twists of the house from above. It felt less surreal to see the sharp, unexpected angles of Amity from this vantage point, a little calmer.

"Have you tried the phone yet?" she asked.

I sucked in my breath. "No," I said shortly. "Why?" There would be check-ins, updates with the doctors at some point, but not yet. And I was

(*slept like the DEAD!*)

fine right now.

Wasn't I?

I squeezed my hands into tight fists, dug my fingernails into the healthy, unmarked flesh of my palms.

I was *fine.*

I am *fine. I am.*

"Oh, it's nothing, really," Ro said, speaking slowly, thoughtfully. "Just that I tried to call yesterday, to see how things were going. But I kept getting a busy signal, like there was something wrong with the line. I wasn't sure if the problems were on my end, or on yours."

"Huh." Had I used the phone yesterday? Had anyone? Had it rung at all? I wasn't sure. "Maybe the phone service isn't hooked up yet. Sometimes things take longer than you expect, I guess especially, you know, out here in no-man's-land."

"Right." Ro shrugged. "But, still. I thought your parents made a point of getting those things taken care of," she said. "For . . . your . . ."

(*slept like the dead*)

"I'm *fine*," I insisted. *Fine*.

Her eyes darted toward my palms, then back to my eyes.

"Okay," she said. "I'm glad." She tilted her head. "But you could tell me if you weren't, you know. You can always tell me."

"I know." I swallowed. My hands pulsed, unseen, throbbing with a ghosted tinge of pain. I shoved them into my back pockets. "But I'm okay. I promise. Come on. I'll show you the rest of the place."

THE SECOND STORY BEHAVED ITSELF for Aunt Ro. The bathroom Luke and I shared betrayed none of the eerie images I'd seen last night, though the mirror was still cracked jaggedly through the middle. If Ro noticed, she didn't mention it. The bedrooms, though still storing pockets of unexpectedly cold air, were unremarkable. Ro commented on the closet space and the original detailing of the claw-foot tub, but beyond that, she was subdued.

As we wound our way to the third floor, a familiar sense of vertigo crept over me. The dimensions of the stairwell seemed to morph and shift the way space had expanded and folded over for me down in the basement. I was woozy as we approached the third-floor landing, and—though it may have been my imagination—Ro appeared to teeter, too. At the top of the staircase, I grabbed the knob of the banister and shut my eyes, willing the floor to steady beneath me. When I opened them again, I painted as bright an expression on my face as possible.

"So. *Ta-da.*" I pretended to curtsy, ignoring the dizziness.

"That was a climb." Ro's face was pale, her upper lip beaded with sweat.

I nodded and winced. "I know, sorry. There's not even much to see up here anyway." The sewing room was behind me, and I gestured to it. "This is the only room we've really used, and just for storage, you know. Stuff we won't need to unpack for a while."

Ro pressed her eyes shut tightly and swayed, leaning against the wall for support.

I moved toward her, tentative. "Do you need to sit down? Are you sure you don't want to rest for a little?" She clearly wasn't quite herself.

Roadblocks, detours, useless directions . . . the phone line being so finicky. It had to be coincidence, all of it. Bizarre, but completely random.

Didn't it?

Ro raised a hand to her mouth. She whispered something, a string of softly breathed syllables I shouldn't have even been able to make out.

Except they'd come from my own lips, too.

"She was shot in the head."

My blood ran cold.

NOW I FELT MORE THAN DIZZY, more than faint. Now I felt as though the floor were slipping out from underneath me, as though Amity's very foundations were crumbling to dust, to ashes, to a gray, papery silt.

Maybe I'd heard her wrong. Maybe the voice had come from inside my

(*crazy*)

head.

"Did you say something, Aunt Ro?" I was quiet, almost as though I didn't actually want her to answer.

Almost.

She whirled to face me, her eyes bloodshot, lined red like road maps. "This house is old, Gwen," she said. Her voice was strained and hoarse. "Very old. It has . . ." She seemed to be struggling for just the right words. " . . . history."

She put a hand on my shoulder. "You're telling me you're feeling good these days? Because I promise, it would be okay if you weren't." Her eyes searched mine. "Your parents, they think the country will be so relaxing, therapeutic. . . . I've heard all of their arguments for moving out here. But being so isolated, it's not for everyone."

"It's quiet," I said.

Quiet out here in the country, that was.

Inside my mind was a different matter entirely. But even with Ro's gaze so imploring, I couldn't admit that.

I had heard my parents' arguments, too. I *was* the argument.

But I was better now. I *was*.

Because I had to be.

Whatever Aunt Ro's suspicions were—however they might have collided with my own nightmares, my own

(*insane*)

fears—I *needed* them to be misguided. Mistaken.

I didn't want to hear any more about Ro's intuitions. Not right now.

Not when it came to me, or to Amity.

RO PAUSED at the door to the sewing room.

I tried not to wonder why, gathering bravado and pushing past her, into the room. I moved—one foot, then the other—and then I was fully inside, just past the threshold. I felt a surge, a twinge of something active and electric, as I stepped in. The air around me seemed to shimmer.

Then I heard the buzzing.

"Gwen?" Ro's voice wobbled, and when I pivoted to look back at her, her eyes were wide and bright, her skin a dull, ashy shade, runny and clammy like something soft left out for too long in the sun.

"Aren't you coming in?" I asked.

The buzzing was louder now, more insistent. I brushed a hand at my ear to no effect. The hum swelled, almost soothing me, lulling me.

"Gwen . . . ," Ro said, her voice watery, unlike anything I'd ever heard from her lips before. "Gwen, I think you should come out of there."

"There's a beautiful view of the river from the window," I insisted, even as the buzzing deepened, twisted, thickened. I moved toward it, waving to her.

Why did it seem so vital, so *crucial*, that Aunt Ro come inside with me? So urgent that she view the Concord River through Amity's windows, through her heavy-framed eyes?

The buzzing was loud as ever by now, and I felt the flicker of tiny beats, tiny bristles against my face.

"*Gwen,*" Ro repeated. She seemed to be almost *shrieking*, her face stretched into a death mask, rubbery with fear. "Come back out of the room. *Now.*"

I squinted. "What's wrong?" She looked sick, but it still wasn't enough to move me—to *remove* me—from the room.

And were those . . . *wings* I felt fluttering at my cheeks? The humming, the buzz, was deafening now, Ro's eyes wide and wild.

I teetered, blinking. The sound, the sensation . . . everything seemed to be multiplying, threatening to fill my nose, my mouth, my ears . . . but I welcomed it.

Then Aunt Ro's hand clamped around my wrist, vise-like, tugging at me. I could almost feel the vacuum-sealed air pop open like a black hole that had suddenly been uncorked.

I opened my mouth wide, to protest, and felt the swarm of insects—*hornets? bees? horseflies?*—rush inside, choking me off, stifling my cries.

Aunt Ro's grip tightened, and I was

(*falling falling falling*)

humming from the inside now, from within and from beneath, from my secret, hidden core.

And then the buzzing silenced, and darkness came down.

"IT DOESN'T MAKE ANY SENSE."

I opened my eyes to the sight of thick, rough-hewn beams overhead—the living room ceiling, if not original to Amity's construction, then at least several centuries old. At the *very* least.

I was on the sofa, stretched on my back, what felt like a pillow propped beneath my head and smelling vaguely of mildew. I swallowed and felt a tightness in my throat, raw and scratchy, and recalled the buzzing of the sewing room, that silent scream, the patter of wings and the creeping cloud of darkness that swarmed around me before blackness came in full.

My mother's voice, slightly muffled. That was what I was hearing. It was coming from the kitchen.

"I'm sorry about the . . . were they *flies?*"

Flies. Yes, in the sewing room. They could have been flies.

I pawed at my neck, pressed my fingers against my throat, searching, trying to ascertain any bites or stings, any telltale swelling. But I could feel nothing but the prickle of goose bumps on my skin.

Ro's voice: a mumble, a low stream of minor chords. Sounds wove in and out from the kitchen, like a radio intermittently losing frequency.

"The window's been open. Who knows how long the realtor left it that way. Could've been all spring, all damn summer. Maybe there was a nest in there, in a closet or a corner or something." My father now, gruff and unyielding.

Ro's voice rose. "Did you *find* a nest, Hal? When you were up there? *Was* the window open?"

There was a banging sound like a knock, or a fist against the surface of a table, and then my father rumbled again, angry and indistinct, that imaginary radio dial shuffling wildly for a moment. Amity's angles were playing tricks on me again. On all of us.

". . . could have opened it and closed it a hundred times just yesterday!" I heard the sound of a chair scraping against the floor, imagined my mother rising to pace the kitchen the way she did when she was anxious. "But I don't see why you should have to *leave* over this. *Flies?* It's ridiculous."

"Insane," my father thundered.

(*crazy*)

My throat lurched. The blood pounded in my ears.

A mumble from Ro. "—didn't see . . . the stings."

"She's *fine!*" my mother shrieked, making my shoulders clench. "There are no marks on her! Or, she *was* fine, until something *you* said got her so upset."

"Let her leave." My father, again.

A door slammed distantly, tinny and thin. It was the screen door off the kitchen. Footsteps grew stronger, drew closer, until Luke's profile passed swiftly by the living room doorway. His hands were curled around something I couldn't make out, and he didn't glance my way. Murray ambled eagerly after him, a whiff of mossy earth, sulfuric and sour, carrying past me in his wake.

There was a ruffle, a scrabbling sound now, slightly frantic, from the kitchen. Aunt Ro: ". . . leave something for Gwen—"

"—you've done enough." An emphatic cough from my father. Another bang, a clap, more like a palm slapped flat against a surface.

Another scraping sound, another chair pushing back from the table. Aunt Ro this time, I thought. "Never mind, I—I guess I didn't bring it with me, after all."

"Ro—" I could picture my mother reaching out, her slim, white arm stretching toward her sister, her forehead creased in concern. "This is all getting bl—"

"—I'll come back soon," Ro said shortly. There was a small hitch in her voice. "But I can't stay tonight. I'm just going to say good-bye to the kids. Then I'm off."

My throat tightened again, swelling hot, tender beneath my fingertips. Faintly, I heard a buzz—just one, simple and razor sharp. I gagged, tried to whisper. Tried to call out, vainly.

I couldn't. The air in Amity was heavy, weighing me down and closing me off, cell by cell.

The darkness came, again.

BUT DOWN IN THE WELL-DEEP BLACK, tucked in some imaginary middle space, Ro's voice came to me. It was warm and slow, like honey. As she spoke, her hair swung against me, brushing my cheek, cocooning me in a silky curtain, reaching me, somehow, even through Amity's murky fog.

"I'm going, Gwen, but I'm here for you." Her words cut channels through the inky distance, tugged at me in my haze.

"You'll let me know if you need anything. Just call for me, and I'll come."

She squeezed my hand.

Through the darkness, I tried to squeeze back.

Moments later, I heard her engine turn over in the driveway, then growl and fade away. My breath came more easily now, improving in slight but steady half measures. The darkness began to lift, to recede.

Of course, it was too late—my breath, the light. I'd lost the chance to say good-bye to Ro.

She was shot in the head, I thought.

She was.

TEN YEARS EARLIER
DAY 3

CONNOR

I LIED ABOUT GOING STRAIGHT HOME EMPTY-HANDED from that shop, our second day at Amity, I mean.

I didn't end up buying anything that would keep the boathouse door closed, that part was the truth, yeah. But another truth was how I hated—always hate—to disappoint Jules. So I didn't come home completely flat-out, bottoms-up empty-handed. Not completely.

I did bring her something back. Just a little dumb nothing piece of junk from a run-down convenience store, no big deal. But that afternoon when I went to give it to her, thinking it would make her smile, or whatever, she and Mom were all caught up putting contact paper on the cabinet shelves. That took about thirty years or so, and then it was more crappy pizza with the slimy canned mushrooms on top that no one likes except Dad, and another night of reading, stuffed up and wrapped like a mummy in my sleeping bag, listening to the firecracker banging from outside, from down by the river.

So that night, I just kept to myself, and waited.

DAY 4

THE FIRST REAL CHANCE I HAD FOR JULES'S LITTLE SURPRISE came the next night. Dad mumbled something about a poker game and tore out after dinner, peeling off down the drive like if he moved fast enough, he could outrun his own shitty soul. Mom tossed the takeout containers—tonight was crappy Chinese instead of crappy pizza for a fun change—and went to give Abel his bath, and then it was just Jules and me, her with some girlie romance book, the kind with loopy silver writing on the cover, as she sprawled out in the sewing room, buried under piles of fuzzy, pilling blankets.

I was pretending to read, flipping the pages of my beat-up paperback back and forth, but the truth was that the brunette had met a real nasty fate a few chapters back, in that elevator scene, and honestly, now it was all getting a little boring.

The story needed more blood, is what I'm saying. I hate being bored.

I was stretched out on the floor, my legs buried under a puddle of blankets so only the holey toes of my socks peeked out. Jules's gift-thing was shoved under the couch I was leaning against, and she was curled up on the saggy cushions above me. The sofa was pushed up opposite a fireplace, and with the way the air was so clammy and cool, I thought a fire would have been nice, like I could even picture the orange glow of the burning wood shining out on us. A fire would go nice at Amity, I thought. But I was too lazy to make one, you know. That night, or any time later. That was kind of too bad.

I wrapped a hand around her leg and she gasped, startled. "Connor!" Her book hit the floor with a dull thud, missing me by an inch or two.

"I got you something." I reached under the sofa and groped for the fuzzy thing, grabbed it, and pushed off my covers, standing. I thrust it at her, all hot and awkward all of a sudden. "It's stupid."

Her face twisted in that confused, surprised look she had, the one that was still happy, even with all of the *what's going on?* underneath. It was a Jules face, one she mostly used with me. Seeing it gave me a small, warm flicker that didn't come too often.

"What is that?" She reached for it, squealing.

I shrugged. "Stuffed dog. From the gas station. The quick mart, you know. Pretty stupid."

Jules loved, I mean, just went totally bonkers-like for dogs. She never really got over it, you know, after Butch died. I always felt kind of bad about that, even though it couldn't be helped.

Even though I never can help myself.

The dog, this little stuffed one, it *was* really stupid. It was small, like the size of an apple, or a little bit bigger, and its fur was white with longer black fuzz at the ears. It wasn't squishy or nice, I mean—it looked and felt like something you'd buy at the convenience store even without counting the nuthouse-green T-shirt it wore, all printed in peeling silkscreen with the logo of a brand of wiper fluid across the front.

"I love him," she said, mouth stretching wide like she meant it, truly. She kissed it on its fake-leather nose.

"Careful. It probably has fleas."

She reached out the hand that was holding it and shoved the toy at my shoulder. "Grouchy Connor. You're such a faker. Everyone knows down deep you're just a big softie."

Well, that wasn't true. But I did have a soft spot for Jules.

"It was nice of you to think of me, bro," she said.

I grunted. "You know."

It didn't happen often—and it especially didn't happen with everyone. But every once in a while, you know, I could be normal. I could be the way other people are all the time. I could be nice.

Once in a while.

DAY 5

I WAS TIRED, LIKE IN THAT WAY THAT YOU FEEL ALL DEEP DOWN IN YOUR BONES, IN YOUR *GUTS*, like they say: *dead* tired, you know? And I for sure wasn't ready to get out of bed. But it looked like I didn't have much say in the matter.

"Connor."

Poke.

Crap.

"Connor."

"Okay! *Jesus.* Okay."

Goddamn Abel. I clenched my fists, tight, the urge to strike making my teeth rattle.

He's only six, I reminded myself.

The thought didn't do too much to kill the twitch in my hands, but I pushed the impulse down as best I could. Tried to bring up that confused-happy face of Jules's from last night again. *Six.*

I thought back to when I was six years old. That's what Jules would have told me to do, what the counselors downstate would've suggested. *Empathize* was their word for it. And even if it didn't exactly come natural to me, I could go through the motions well enough. When I felt like it.

Draw on a memory, they'd say. *Find something real.*

Six. There are things I remember about being six years old, sure. Some specific things, real things. Stuff I'd rather not talk about, mostly.

But, you couldn't compare—I was never anything like Abel. Not even back then.

Probably a good thing for Abel.

I flipped to my side, away from the stark bedroom wall, and sat up, folding back the corner of my sleeping bag and squinting. What time *was* it anyway? That sunlight was blinding.

It took another minute or two, but when my eyes could finally focus, there was Abel—no big surprise—shifting back and forth, nervous and twitchy, at the foot of the bed. His pajama pants sagged at the knees so he seemed even younger than he was. Smaller. Vulnerable, I mean.

But that didn't change the fact that he woke me up, on purpose. My temper flared, no matter how I tried to remember *six years old* and stuff.

"You know you're not supposed to bother me, especially first thing in the morning." That was something my brother learned early on. The hard way.

He opened his mouth, then closed it again.

"What is it?" I asked, louder. *Why can't you just SPIT IT OUT?* I wanted to shout. I bit my tongue, almost hard enough to draw blood, like wanting to taste it, even.

"I'm hungry." His eyes were round.

Hungry. That coppery blood taste in my mouth. It wasn't real, I knew. Where did it come from? "Why didn't you wake Mom? Or Jules?"

He shrugged. "I tried. Mommy wouldn't get up."

Well, fine. Sometimes that happened. Fair enough. She

wasn't exactly a stranger to the wonders of modern medicine, and if she took something to help her sleep last night, she was probably all six feet deep in the Valley of the Dolls right about now.

"And Jules's door is locked."

Now I sat up real straight, peering at Abel. He wasn't the hardiest kid, you know—not the most resilient, I mean—but he wasn't *slow* or anything like that. So him saying that Jules had locked her door—that was weird. *Really* weird.

Because none of the bedrooms in Amity had locks on their doors.

I'd checked right away when we first arrived. Privacy is important to me, for a lot of reasons, you know. The boathouse door wasn't the only one constantly hanging half open. I *knew* the bedrooms didn't have locks. But whatever the kid may miss here and there, I mean, Abel wasn't a liar. He wasn't lying now. I would know, too—I could usually spot a lie from ten feet away.

"Her door can't be locked, Abe." I swung around on the bed and stood.

"But it is," he said, like, *well, that's that*, which I guess it was to him.

"Nope. No locks," I insisted, moving across the floor, out the door, and down the hall to Jules's room. Abel padded after me. I could tell he was working up to one of his righteous fits for if—*when*—he was proven wrong. I was actually sort of looking forward to it. "Look."

I reached out, grabbed Jules's doorknob.

I twisted it and shoved my weight forward.

The doorknob rattled in my hand. But it didn't turn, didn't spring open like it should have.

Like it *would* have.

If it weren't locked.

I had one of those rare flashes of annoyance at Jules. Mainly I was jealous she figured out a way to jam her door-knob when I should have been the one to come up with that first. If I had, I'd be the one still asleep instead of standing, dumbly, in my sweatpants, waiting for the *I-told-you-so* smile to appear on Abel's face.

But Abel knew better than that. He also knew better than to say out loud, *Well?* Though he was thinking it hard enough that it was all either of us could hear.

I glared at him. "I don't know," I said, running my fingers through my hair. "It didn't have a lock on it before." Because it *didn't*. I'd checked it. I would have known. Would have seen.

I mean, I notice those kinds of things.

I pressed my index fingers against my temples and closed my eyes for a minute. Why was it so *bright* in the hallway? I opened them to see Abel grinning up at me. I wanted to smack him. Or worse. That sharp, metal taste filled up my mouth, again.

"I don't know, Abel," I said again. "Maybe it stuck in the humidity. Wood can warp in the heat, you know?"

But we both knew that was just some dumb explanation, like grown-ups make for things they can't explain.

"Maybe," Abel agreed, his eyes saying otherwise, and again I wanted to reach out and . . . *something*.

Something not good.

I tried to push the thought back.

"Go wash up." I choked back all the ugly things I really wanted to say to him right then. "I'll fix you some cereal."

Anything to get out of that hall, away from Jules's door and the way it was mocking me. I could've tried going through the bathroom to get to her—should have, maybe—but by then the bloody, coppery taste running down my throat was strong enough so all I wanted was to get down to the kitchen and wash it down with a glass of water, or something.

Abel didn't move, and the urge to rage at him, to scream and lash out, it rushed at me again. It was just so *bright* there in the hallway. Like crazy-making bright. A person couldn't be expected to behave rationally with that kind of, I don't know, unearthly *glow* going on. "Come on."

He balked. "I don't want to."

"Too bad." Life was full of disappointing lessons, and I could teach him all about those. I didn't want to spend one more second in that hallway. The sunlight streaming in from the stained glass at the end of the hall was like a laser. For a minute, I wondered if it could actually cut straight through me. For a minute, I thought that wouldn't be so weird, so impossible, I mean, here in this place. *"Go."*

He made a face. "The bathroom . . . smells," he offered finally. "I don't like it."

Jesus. "It's a *bathroom*," I pointed out. "It's not going to smell like roses."

Abel shifted. "Not like . . . not like that," he said. "There's a . . . there's a *way*, a way that it smells. Like . . . like something awful."

Blood. On my tongue, in my throat, rushing through me like electricity. "It's a *bathroom*."

"It smells like something . . . bad. Like something *wrong*," he insisted. "I don't like it."

115

The redness flared behind my eyelids again, and I actually, physically, felt my body twitch, pitch toward him, wanting to reach out, to twist and crunch and—

But that was an *overreaction*, what the school counselor back downstate would have called a *distortion*. Abel was six. Just a kid. All he was doing was behaving like a six-year-old kid.

It was a bathroom. It smelled weird. No big deal, right? There was no godly reason in the world that my nerve endings should be humming like they were exposed, like my skin'd been peeled back in one long yank, like I was standing here, in the searing light of this hallway, with my insides on the outside, raw and runny.

I counted to three.

"It's just a bathroom, Abel." I forced each word past the edges of my teeth. "Maybe the pipes are rusted or something. But you still have to wash up. *Now.*"

"I—" I could tell he was thinking about protesting again, but the look on my face must have changed his mind. "Fine." He shuffled toward the bathroom like a death row inmate, shoulders slumped, staggering slightly.

I gagged and swallowed that make-believe bucket of blood back down.

I MADE IT MAYBE ALL OF TEN FEET DOWN THE HALL BEFORE ABEL SCREAMED, loud enough to rattle my bones and then some. Truly, the last time I could recall hearing a sound like that coming out of that kid was when he was four and dislocated his shoulder after he was caught messing around in Dad's tool kit. Dad wasn't too happy about that, don't you know.

I froze in the hallway, thinking that his banshee-scream would probably wake the others, so I wouldn't have to deal with him and his stupid breakfast after all. Or if he woke Dad, there'd be worse stuff to deal with than Abel's breakfast. But even after a beat or two, no one came—weird, really weird— and holy *God*, the screeching wasn't quieting down at all.

So I doubled back into the bathroom to see what was going on.

I DON'T KNOW WHAT I EXPECTED TO FIND WHEN I GOT THERE—I guess I'd already decided that the godforsaken screaming was just Abel being a freak—so I for sure wasn't prepared to peep into the doorway and see him crouched, tucked under the sink, rocking on the tiled floor, knees pulled up to his chest, bawling away.

"What the *hell*, Abel?" I asked, leaning down and reaching an arm out to pull him up.

He swatted me away and shrieked even louder. "I *told* you I don't like it in here," he gasped between sobs. "I *told* you."

I grabbed at his wrists and dragged him to his feet. "Yeah, you told me. And I told *you* you were being crazy. So quit it right now." I glanced around the bathroom. "There's nothing in here to be afraid of. Unless you've got some hang-up about ugly vinyl shower curtains. So get over it."

He rubbed at his snotty nose with the back of his hand. "It's blood," he muttered.

Blood?

I could still taste it in the back of my throat. The thing about blood is: it's one of those *real*, tactile things that ground me, I've been told. And not in a good way. Blood made this moment, this situation, a little more interesting. Especially with the imaginary tang of it still coating my tongue.

"What are you talking about, Abel? Did you hurt your-self?" I reached for his hand again, but he pulled back.

He shook his head, real resolved-like. "Not me. Not *my* blood."

"Where?" A look around the room told me he was either seeing things, or just plain lying. *Oh come on.* That voice inside me was real steady, real sure. *Come* on.

"The sink." He kept his gaze on the floor like his head was glued that way. "When I tried to run the taps."

I sighed. "It's an old house, Abel. The pipes are probably rusty. What you saw was probably rust. Not blood." Of *course*, whatever it was that he saw, it wasn't blood. Of course not. *Come. ON.*

Never mind what you *saw in the window that night, Connor.*

Because I was different, right? I *am* different. The way that I see things—the things that I see—they aren't the same things that normal people see.

"Look." I grabbed him by the shoulders and turned him so he was facing the basin, so he couldn't look away, forcing his clenched fists back down to his sides. I took his face be-tween my palms and swiveled it, enjoying—I have to admit this now—the pulse of his skinny neck tendons. *"Look."*

I twisted the cold water tap.

For a minute, nothing happened. Like, nothing at all, not even that gassy little puff of stale air that coughs up when old plumbing gets goosed after years of no use. I'd been so ready for a thick stream of metallic liquid that the empty moment felt swollen, full-up with badness, or something like. I held my breath, fixed on the tap, wondering if it actually *was* blood that was going to come rushing out.

119

Wondering if I wanted it to be.

I exhaled slow, and then there was a giant, creaking groan, and a gush of putrid . . . *sludge*, that was really the best word for it, a brownish *sludge* that came streaming down in heavy chunks, filthy rainfall that was halfway between a liquid and a solid, really.

Whatever it was, it definitely wasn't *blood*—blood wasn't thick and clotted that way, I knew, not when it was running fresh—but this *was* repulsive. Completely disgusting, like last night's leftovers run through the garbage disposal, taking a brief curtain call on their way to the town's sewer system.

My stomach hitched, and I closed my eyes, trying not to react. Whatever was coming out of that tap was nasty, for sure, but it wasn't *blood*, and I'd be damned if I was going to feed Abel's little freak-out.

But . . . that *smell* . . . it was awful. That image of trash collecting in a drain came back to me, and I shuddered, my stomach flipping over again. The taste of blood was gone from my mouth and I actually wanted it back just then, like truly wished for it, is how bad whatever was coming out of the sink was.

All of a sudden, that image came back to me—a shotgun again, like the one I saw in that creepy half vision, half dream that first night. The one that appeared with the banging of the boathouse door, I mean. There wasn't any banging in the bathroom—there wasn't any sound except for pipes creaking and Abel bawling and the hiccupping gushes belching from the faucet—but I saw that shotgun just the same, and caught a whiff of gunpowder under all the stinking rot filling up the room. I pressed the heels of my palms against my eyes, but it didn't make the image go away.

"See?" Abel tugged at the hem of my shorts. "See what I mean? It's *blood*."

Oh, I saw all right. It wasn't blood, but it was *awful*, reeking of decay and dripping with . . . I didn't even want to guess. I could see it clear as I could see my own hand in front of my face. Clear as I'd seen that shriveled, stripped-down corpse—*because, yeah, let's just say it, that's what it was, what I saw*—in the window that first night.

But it still wasn't blood. And I couldn't let Abel know how, whatever it *was*, it was making me want to crawl right out of my skin. I was having another *overreaction*, and I couldn't let it show.

We had to get out of that room. The stink was making me swoon.

"It's not blood, Abel." A fresh wave of dizziness hit me as I forced the words out. "I told you. It's an old house; the plumbing is funky. Probably the pipes are half rotted out—" I tripped on that word *rotted*, because, man, that was exactly what the room smelled like.

"That's probably why we could even afford this place. Why it was so cheap. I bet the pipes are nothing but mold and rust." And, man, oh man, why did that image make me think of a human being, a human body, all blood and guts, veins and insides? Why did it make me think of that yawning mouth, those eyeless sockets, all peering out at me from the window?

Why would mold, and rust, and rot suggest *bodies*—I caught myself. "It's not *blood*, Abel. Jesus. Quit being such a baby. Just brush your teeth in the kitchen sink. And forget about it." That's what I was going to do anyway.

Rusty pipes. That was all it was. Nothing to be afraid of.

Not for me.

NOW

DAY 6

GWEN

THE AIR AROUND AMITY WAS UNRELIABLE. By day, the August heat shimmered off the surface of the Concord River. But at night, chill slithered down over us, so dense it seemed to streak the walls. Country living, Mom said, though I didn't think she really believed that.

At night, Luke would wander the house draped under a ratty afghan he said he'd found in the cellar. Mom muttered something about fleas, prompting Dad to fiddle with the thermostat mounted on the living room wall.

It made no difference. "Broken," Dad decided. "Part of why the place was so cheap."

Luke pointed out the fireplace in the living room. *Why not?*

Why not mainly had to do with our family being totally and completely unprepared for rural life; my parents had fallen in love with Amity, but hadn't considered where, exactly, we were moving to. We hadn't bought any firewood. It was August, after all. So fireplace or no, there was nothing to burn.

"There's an ax," Luke had said. "Outside. And a woodpile. All we need to do is split the logs."

"Is that all?" I tried to keep my voice light.

Mom made some clucking sounds about axes being dangerous, which I had to agree with. But Luke was determined, and that seemed to be the end of that.

If not the end of the bitter, frigid nights.

DAYTIME AT AMITY, THOUGH . . . daytime was a completely different story.

Daytime at Amity, at least that first week of August, was stagnant, lulling me into a state of suspended animation, unable to focus on more than the most distilled, deliberate thought for any real length of time. In the heat, my mind felt slippery and loose, my breath—so vivid and sharp in the chill of the deep night—a shallow pull that never seemed to quite slide down past the lump always expanding in my throat.

I thought that daytime at Amity was starting to make me crazy.

By my sixth day, I had to do something about it. Beautiful as the view was from our back porch, I needed to do something other than sit out there, motionless, baking in the sun. It felt, out there, like my brain was melting, like my skin was deteriorating from the heat, separating from my bones. It felt, out there, like *I* was deteriorating. Pulling apart, repelling, like oil and water.

I couldn't let that happen. Couldn't fall apart.

Not again.

IT WAS A RIVER, AFTER ALL, so swimming seemed like a logical antidote to the suffocating heat. So logical I couldn't believe I hadn't thought of it sooner. The heat truly was affecting my reason.

The boathouse had become Luke's domain; he disappeared into it for hours at a time. He was cleaning it out, he said, clearing up refuse left in the previous owners' wake, and suggested the rest of us keep our distance until he'd finished.

Recalling the ominous shotgun sound of the boathouse doors our first night at Amity,

(she was shot in the head)

I was happy to oblige. Luke claimed the rickety shed held a leaky old rowboat he'd never trust to stay afloat, much less propel a person from one point to another. But more promising to me just then; it had a dock, solid looking enough despite the mossy undergrowth of algae clinging to its pilings.

Swimming it was, then.

I FOUND LUKE AROUND THE SIDE OF THE HOUSE, framed neatly between the two half-moon eyes of Amity's attic windows. He hovered over the base of a thick tree trunk, contemplating an ax buried in the worn, ringed surface of the wood. The ax itself was unremarkable, embedded maybe a quarter inch deep into the tree trunk, blade scarred with rust. The look on my brother's face was more unsettling than anything else about the scene. Beside him, Murray stood, hackles on edge, a low growl caught in his throat.

Something about the glaze to Luke's eyes made me wonder how long he'd been standing out there, in that very position. *Too long,* I thought. My typically easy, good-natured brother looked two-dimensional and sepia toned in the unrelenting afternoon light.

The heat, I told myself.

"What are you doing?" I asked, hating the lilt in my voice.

He twitched like I'd startled him. Taking me in, he stepped back from the ax, as if deliberately distancing himself. "Gwen. Sorry. I didn't see you come up."

"Clearly," I said, glad just then that the ax was firmly lodged in the tree trunk, and not swinging from my brother's hands. "So?"

He stretched. "Firewood. Like we talked about."

I almost laughed. "*Like we talked about.* Yeah, we talked about it. But I thought we all voted that idea down." It occurred to me to bring up the dining room, the twisted, ruined nails, and that deep, hollow echo from within the walls . . . and then it occurred to me not to.

Then I did laugh, nervously. Luke didn't notice, which was unusual for him. He raised his hand up, shielding his eyes from the sun, and nodded toward a stack of wood resting alongside the wall of the house. "We've got too much now to let it go to waste. It's nice and dry; should burn well. Really, I just need to split it."

"*Really.*" I choked back a

(*hysterical*)

strangled sound and pushed the echoes from my head, denied that clipped, portentous *slam-click-BANG* that flared in my ears, my throat, my chest,

(*she was shot in the head*)

as I envisioned blade splitting grain, slicing and paring with keen, brutal precision.

Finally, he looked truly, directly *at* me. His eyes were narrow slits. "Yeah," he said, curt. "That's all."

Murray whimpered and curled himself into a tight ball beside the woodpile. "Great, okay. If you think so." I tried to sound casual.

"The house is freezing at night," he said shortly. "We need to do something about it."

I shivered, wanting to change the subject. I remembered, suddenly, what I had come outside for in the first place.

"I'm going for a swim. Do you want to come? The wood will still be here when we get back."

Luke didn't register that I'd spoken at all. Again, his gaze had fixed on the handle of the ax, and the fault line in the tree trunk's base where the blade had penetrated.

"No thanks," he said finally, the words oozing from his mouth.

I struggled to keep my voice even. "You're not going to start with this now, though? Right? You'll pass out from sunstroke."

"What?" He shook his head. He sounded confused, fuzzy.

"You'll wait before you even pick up that ax," I clarified. "Right?" Murray made a snuffling sound, as though agreeing with me, and shifted the fold of his front paws.

Luke shrugged. "I don't know."

"Come down to the dock if you change your mind," I said lamely.

"Maybe. I guess." Luke scratched at his chin. He was looking at the ax, again. "The blade needs to be sharpened," he decided. "Yeah."

Murray jumped up and darted behind me, ears flattened against his head. Luke stepped forward and curled a fist around the handle of the ax, and Murray yelped as though my brother had grabbed him by the tail.

"Oh, um, Luke, that's—"

That's a bad idea. I flinched instinctively. Luke didn't notice. He pumped the ax handle once or twice, his elbow clenching, his face contorted.

It's not going to come out, I hoped. *It won't.*

I reached a hand out to Luke, and felt a—a *twinge,* some sort of internal *charge,* like my organs had been electrocuted.

Luke grunted. He braced his legs and yanked. The electric

sensation danced down my spine. The ax blade wavered in the wood, then rocked, finally dislodging.

With one arm, Luke swung it wide, arcing the ax broadly over his shoulder. My teeth clamped together with the force of a door slamming. I tottered backward, tripping over a shivering Murray.

"Are you *crazy?*" I rasped. "What if that thing went flying? You could have killed someone."

You could have killed me.

Luke turned to look at me blankly. "But I didn't," he said, toneless. "You're fine."

I didn't *feel* fine. Not at all.

I untangled myself from Murray, patting him reassuringly. Now I was eager to make space between myself and my brother. "Anyway, I'm going. Swimming."

Luke didn't answer. He was preoccupied again, toying with the ax, turning it from side to side.

"This needs to be sharpened," he mumbled.

"It looks plenty sharp to me."

Luke ignored me. I headed back inside the house, Murray close at my heels.

IT DIDN'T TAKE ME LONG TO CHANGE INTO MY SWIMSUIT, eager as I was to shake off my exchange with Luke outside.

As usual, once I was inside, it was easier to shrug off my own jerky, birdlike timidity, easy to see my own trembling responses as an overreaction. As what the doctors might call a *heightened state, hysteria.*

For axes to make me jumpy was fine—it probably wasn't all that unusual as far as human behavior went—but, I'd brought more than my fair share of

(*crazy*)

swirling, nervous energy to that conversation by the woodpile.

A swim would do me good, clear my head.

Mom told me that most of the beach towels were still packed away, piled in the boxes cluttering up the third-floor sewing room. No one had ventured inside it since Ro's visit, but my father insisted it'd been purged of any infestation. I had no memory of being stung and Ro's hushed good-bye felt like little more than a waking dream. I took the spiral staircase two steps at a time, the prospect of that first, crisp slice through the river driving me up and around, up and around.

Up and around.

Up. And around.

Up.

And around.

And around.

The heat rose with me. By the time I reached the third-story landing, clinging to the banister, the blood pounded against my temples, pulsing waves of vivid red that radiated down my spine. I could feel my heartbeat in my fingertips, in the curve of my lower belly, under the soft padding of my toes.

I could feel *her*. Amity.

I wasn't alone at the top of the staircase. Amity was with me, enveloping every open space, every cell of my self. And she was playing tricks on me.

All at once, Amity's staircase was like a hall of mirrors. My heartbeat, the rhythm of my breathing, the shadowy atmo-sphere dancing across my bare, exposed thighs—they all knew it to be true, even as my mind insisted it couldn't possibly be.

Amity was like a fun house—all odd, cockeyed angles and unexpected edges. It stood only three stories high (not in-cluding that cavernous cellar), but as I wound my way up the staircase, it suddenly seemed to go on forever, narrowing to an infinite horizon with each step I climbed.

Amity was playing tricks on me.

But, no. That was *hysteria*, again. A *heightened state* brought on by lack of oxygen, by taking the twisting, rickety staircase too quickly. It had to be.

What would happen if I were to retreat, shrieking, back down the staircase, thrash wildly through the house, calling for my mother, insisting there was something outright *wrong, sentient, aware* . . .

. . . something outright *evil* about this place?

What then?

Well. I knew *what then*, didn't I?

Then came the doctors, soft-spoken and sympathetic, pens tapping at notebooks, nods and murmurs and unconvincing reassurances. *Then* came hushed conferences with my mother and father, concerned glances, prescription pads. *Then* came pills: flat tablets and chubby capsules, bitter aftertaste and chalky residue.

Then came the fitful place between wake and dream, where I was never quite lucid, never quite sure even of my physical presence. Never quite sure where my own thoughts ended and everything else began.

Then came hospitals. Treatments, therapies, needles . . . and the crushing, overwhelming futility of trying to assert my own jagged, fractured perspective. The futility of trying to convince people.

That was the reason that Amity couldn't be *aware*, couldn't be involved, invested in me.

Couldn't be *alive*.

That just wasn't the way things worked.

THE ONLY CHOICE, THEN, WAS TO DENY; to squeeze my eyes shut and insist, *insist* to myself that the twisted, menacing proportions of the third floor, of Amity, were not some slick, calibrated trick of the paranormal, but only a glitch, a hiccup, of my own mind. To *insist* against the whispers rustling in my ear, so ominously similar to Ro's twilight-state farewell.

Against the distant, faint buzz of insects, swarming, invisible, just above the surface of my skin.

It's only a hallway, Gwen, I insisted.

Only a house.

THE SEWING ROOM WAS DUSTY, strung with cobwebs and speckled with particles that drifted in and out of the sunlight, a prism of neglect. But nothing about the room was particularly otherworldly. The buzzing sound had stopped.

Thankfully, it took only a quick scan of the boxes to locate the one labeled BEACH TOWELS in my mother's neat, efficient scrawl. After a brief tussle with a length of packing tape, I fished one out, a swath of vivid Day-Glo stripes that defied the darker murmurings of my mind.

Thank goodness.

Vaguely calmed, I slung the towel over my shoulder and moved closer to the large, multi-paned picture window on the far wall of the room. The view truly *was* a portrait: bold, verdant foliage rioting against the cloudless sky. The river beckoned to me.

But . . .

I blinked and leaned closer to the smudged glass. *The wind must be rustling the trees,* I told myself. *Surely that's all that's out there.*

It was the first, the best explanation. The sensible, reasonable, *rational* explanation.

But it wasn't the *right* one.

That's not the wind, Gwen.

There was someone *out* there. Down by the boathouse. A young girl, maybe ten years old, a blur in faded jeans and a wild, thick ponytail that danced back and forth over her shoulders as she moved.

Who *was* she?

I sighed.

Slowly, like an unexpected kiss, I felt a firm hand slip around my waist. The gesture was soothing, reassuring. Comforting.

And then there was my mother, the scent of her freesia hand lotion enveloping me, and her breath on my cheek.

"What are you looking at, Gwen?" she asked.

"There's . . . Did you see someone out there?" I pointed to the spot where I'd seen the girl only seconds before, but she'd vanished in the split second I'd let my attention wander.

"I saw your brother outside with the ax. It looks like he's really planning to cut some firewood. Why do I feel like that's something I should discourage?"

I didn't want to think about Luke, about the ax. The girl's image had grounded me, and I wanted to cling to that.

"Never mind," I said, shrugging. I turned from the window at last . . .

. . . and stopped, stock-still.

My mother stood in the doorway of the sewing room.

My mother stood, head cocked slightly, looking quizzical, in the doorway of the sewing room.

She wasn't directly behind me, although I'd felt her breath on the nape of my neck, and sensed her skin by its smell . . .

. . . and felt her arm at my waist.

She hadn't been behind me at all.

She'd been standing in the doorway of the sewing room.

My mother had been standing, not behind me, but in the doorway of the sewing room.

She'd been standing in the doorway of the sewing room this whole time.

TEN YEARS EARLIER
DAY 8

SUNDAY WAS PRETTY QUIET, for a change.

Mom went to church, like usual. She'd always been pretty into religion and stuff; I guess her family was like that when she was growing up, I mean. We didn't see her family too much—they were settled further up the coast, and I guess they weren't too fond of Dad, which I couldn't exactly blame them for.

So it was Sunday, and it was quiet. Mom was at Mass, and Jules was somewhere in the house watching Abel, and Dad was down by the boathouse, working on this beat-up Leeward, a day sailer he scavenged as soon as he'd signed the papers on Amity. He'd always wanted to have a boat, he'd said. *Always.* It was the first any of us were hearing about this lifelong dream.

The thing was a real clunker anyway—you could see just from looking at it; it was old enough that it was wood, not fiberglass, and no joke, that wood had seen better days. You didn't have to know anything about boats to know that it would be a long time before this one was ready to test its sea legs again. Even in the hands of someone who knew what he was doing, and that wasn't really Dad. Okay, he was mechanical—always real hands-on at the dealership—but boats were never his specialty.

But it kept him busy, so I wasn't complaining.

Honestly, it was actually starting to feel maybe a little *too* quiet around the house. Boring. And if there's one thing I hate, it's being bored. I'm not real good with boredom. That was one thing the counselors downstate would say, over and over, and as far as that went, I had to agree with them.

Mom'd got it together to stand up for herself enough so now there was a cheap-ass phone in the kitchen again, plugged in, just waiting, *lurking*-like, you know, in case there was ever some kind of emergency.

I picked it up to dial someone, just for something to do. I don't even know who I was thinking I'd call—it's not like I had this great crowd of friends back downstate, just waiting to hear how I was doing, you know?

'Course nothing can ever be easy with Dad. So even though there was a phone and it was plugged in, I guess we weren't up-to-date on the bills, because when I picked up the receiver, all I heard was a shaky static that put my teeth on edge. It was as bad as nails on a chalkboard, or the whispers that sometimes come to me from inside my own messed-up head.

Faulty wiring: my brain. The phone. Tons of things in my life.

I slammed down the phone, but the whispers didn't stop. There was still that rustling, like a fire burning somewhere. My skin felt real itchy, like it was suddenly the wrong size for my body. Sometimes that happens to me.

Anyway, I was feeling real bored, twitchy, buzzing from wanting to be distracted.

I needed to move.

SECONDS, MINUTES, HOURS, WEEKS later, I blinked, and I was there, at the top of the basement stairs.

And now I heard music. It was coming from below, full of static, like an out-of-range radio station.

The door, heavy and wooden and thick, was closed. When I reached for the handle, it resisted.

Amity and her locks. As the music swelled in my head, I slammed forward hard with all of my body weight, imagining the door splintering from its hinges, imagining me riding it like a sled, down the staircase, into the black. I saw this so clear I was sure, like completely certain it would happen, that I'd just go flying, riding that door like a magic carpet, empty hinges squeaking in my wake.

But the door didn't break open.

Instead, I heard a click, like a key turning in a lock.

The doorknob twisted, and that basement door swung open.

IT WAS DARK DOWNSTAIRS, and then the music trailed off, so I was alone with my wet, raggedy breathing.

I reached out and groped along, moving forward best as I could in that thick darkness. The walls were damp and I smelled must, stone, and dirt, and underneath that, a spoiled smell, like rotting. That death-shroud, coffin feeling from the first night came back to me. I wiggled my fingers just to prove to myself that I could, that I was actually here, that I was real. That I was alive.

The wall moved.

I wiggled my fingers again, stronger now. My hand closed over a smooth, oval stone. It was big, like an egg that something prehistoric—something make-believe, I mean—would leave behind.

I wondered just for a minute if this was one of those times the counselors warned me about. A *distortion*, one of those time-space hiccups that swept me away from now, from all of the rest of the world.

The counselors don't like those hiccups, what they do to me. What they mean for everyone else.

But there weren't any counselors here right now. Just me.

Me and Amity.

I flexed my fingers and shoved my hand further, pushed

that giant rock so it rattled, so it shifted a little in place.

Is there . . .

Is there something behind the wall? I rapped a fist against the rocks, but it was hard to hear an echo with the basement walls all mossy and damp. I clamped my fingers around the egg, twisting it, stretched as far up on my toes as I could go in that grave-like space. . . .

There was a scraping sound, and the little hitch of resistance coming undone. My stomach squeezed, excited-like.

Almost . . .

I heard a scream.

RAGE, THAT GREAT OLD FRIEND OF MINE, STABBED AT ME, HOT AND SHARP, in a way that I liked as much as I didn't.

It rushed at me, so I snapped, all sudden, back to that real-Real place, the one where other people live, where the buzzing in my head is—mostly—dim enough that those screams—*those screams!*—could break through.

Abel.

Wasn't Jules watching him?

I moved, reluctant first, then faster as the wails started building some serious steam, bounding up the basement stairs like a maniac. I thought if Abel was bawling about the crap in the bathroom pipes again, I'd slap him so hard his teeth rattled.

I thought: *I'll give him a real reason to cry.*

But upstairs, the bathroom was empty, and the doors to the bedrooms were all closed. Confused, I took a minute to pinpoint where the noise—tapering down a little bit—was really coming from.

The river?

Yeah. The river. That kind of made sense for some reason, didn't it?

I whipped back through the house, winding from the dining room to the kitchen, running up to the sink and leaning against it, searching, a little bit frantic, out the wide back window.

That was when the music started again.

It was broken and choppy, clouding up all the space in my head like a warning signal, or something stronger, even. And when I glanced down at the river, past the low, hilly slope of our backyard, it was running red.

Blood red.

"CONNOR."

Rage needled me again *(oh hey, buddy—how's it goin'?)*, and *wham!*—there I was, back in the kitchen, the Concord River churning along, back to its normal, muddy-river-water color now.

And I *knew* it was normal, that color; I mean, I knew it was the way all of those regular, normal people saw the river when they looked at it. But buried down deep, I had this strong, solid feeling that actually the blood was the true part, the *real*-Real, if that makes any sense.

I don't know. I guess it's kind of confusing, where Amity ends and everything else begins.

But it made sense to me, that I'd be the only one to pick up on that, the only person to see the bloody water with my own two stupid eyes. It went along with most of what I'd come to know about myself, what I'd come to teach other people about who I truly am.

Even though the river was back to so-called "normal," there was still, for sure, a flash of blazing blood red happening in the corner of my eyes. And when I turned toward it, toward the sound of my name, there was Jules, curls in crazy corkscrews down her shoulders, hands on her hips, looking maybe annoyed, maybe even something worse.

A trickle of blood ran from her nose.

"What happened?" I asked, and I could have meant a million different things.

"Abel went down to the boathouse," she said. Her jaw was tight. "He wanted to check it out."

She reached for an almost-used-up roll of paper towels on the counter. I pulled a sheet off for her, folded it into a square, and ran it under some water from the tap, that stinking sulfur smell hanging in the air between us. She tilted her head back and I stepped toward her, pressing the towel against the trail of blood oozing from her nose. Honestly, I was kind of mesmerized by it. I *wanted* to get closer to that red rivulet.

I *liked* it. Even though I didn't like to see Jules hurt.

"And the screaming?" I asked.

She shook her head. "The door swung shut on him, caught his fingers pretty badly. I had to tape them up. Luckily, Dad had a first-aid kit down there."

"So what happened to *you*?" I waved at her nose, like she needed a reminder.

She shrugged, uncomfortable. "That's the weird thing. When I got to the boathouse, Abel was freaking out. Completely losing it. The door had closed on him, and when I asked about it, he went on and on about how it had closed on him *on purpose.*

"Like something *deliberately* closed his fingers in the door. Pinning him inside."

She bit her lip, like she was waiting for me to burst out laughing, right in her face. But as she was speaking, that tinny, faraway music was building in my head again. And that shaking, live-wire feeling in my stomach was telling me:

Something *had* tried to hurt Abel.

She was right.

"CONNOR,"

Jules said again, with more edge this time, and nasal, too, what with how the paper towel was pressed up against one nostril. The white square was blooming a watery pink that looked almost pretty—sort of delicate—in the afternoon light.

"Yeah?" I felt all clouded over again. *Did she notice?*

Of course she does. It's Jules.

"God, what is *with* you these days?" she said. "You're on another planet. *More* on another planet than usual," she corrected herself. She tossed the wadded paper towel to the counter, where it sat, looking like a squashed, bled-out gerbil against the linoleum, and pinched the bridge of her nose.

"The door closed on Abel's fingers on purpose. Is what you were saying." My voice was dull, but I could still, you know, form the words, could repeat her story back to her.

She sighed. "Well, that's what he said. And, obviously, I told him that was ridiculous." She hunched her shoulders. "But here's the thing. . . ."

My pulse began to hammer, like started to really whale against my ribs.

"When I went to open the door again, after I'd got in there, and had a look at Abel's hand? The door wouldn't open. Like Abel said. It wouldn't go."

"It was stuck."

"I mean, yes, I'm sure that's all it was, that it was stuck. Wood warps and all that. But, I'm telling you, Connor—" She lowered her voice, like whatever she was going to say was some huge secret and not just exactly something I already knew, something I was already feeling with every square inch of my body. "It didn't *feel* like warped wood." She shuddered. "It felt like there was someone—some*thing*—on the other side of the door, blocking it.

"Keeping us locked inside."

She folded her arms across her chest, like a challenge.

I locked eyes with her, and my spine hummed.

Real, I thought. *Real.*

In my mind, I saw the Concord River, rushing, churning red.

THE GRUMBLE OF MOM'S BEATER SEDAN CHOKING TO A STOP IN THE DRIVEWAY snapped us both from our mini-trances.

"So, what about your nose anyway?" I asked while I fumbled with the dirty paper towel. I tossed it in the trash bin under the sink. A puff of rotten-fruit stench drifted up from the cabinet before it shut again, sealing up all the nasty, grimy bits of trash tight. Everything in this house stank like rot.

And I liked it.

"Dad heard Abel screaming, the door banging. He pulled on the door so when it opened, it swung back and hit me in the face. I'm telling myself it was an accident, although he didn't bother to apologize." She tapped her first finger against her nostrils real sensitive, tentative. "I think it's stopped now. I'm fine."

Anger surged through my limbs.

"I'm sorry I didn't get outside in time," I said, feeling honestly, truly sorry, because, I mean: who knows? Maybe I could have stopped Dad. Or maybe I *could* have done something to get the door open, get Abel out, before anything went haywire to begin with.

Yeah, I thought I could have found a way to get the door open. I thought that might be what all of that music, all of that echo in my chest might've meant. That I maybe had an *in* with . . . well, with Amity. Some kind of all-access pass.

But I'd been busy. Too busy to hear, to notice, down there in the cellar.

"What were you doing anyway?" Jules asked. Her voice got scratchy and kind of high-pitched. "And what the hell happened to your *hands*, Connor? Where were you?"

I looked down. My hands hung limp at my sides, like slabs of meat, like someone else's body parts.

They were caked in dirt. *Covered.* Like I hadn't been just scrabbling down in the basement's stone walls, but had been knee-deep out by the riverbank, clawing at the earth like a wild animal or something.

I didn't notice before, and I guess Jules was too focused on her nose to see it, either. I still had that huge, round stone in my hand. It looked like something from medieval times, from a castle, or maybe a fort. Some place strong and closed off, I mean.

"I got dirty" was all I could think to say.

"DO YOU KNOW WHAT THAT IS?"

She meant the stone, obviously, from the way those little gold sparks in her eyes had caught on it, were scanning it all intense-like. She gnawed away on her lower lip.

"A rock." Even though I definitely knew, definitely had a feeling, that it was more than that. Special, in some way. Meant for me.

She rolled her eyes and made that cute exasperated face she loved to give me. "Right, ten points, brain trust. But a rock, a stone that size—that shape . . . Where did you find it?"

"In the cellar."

She shook her head like a little thrill had just passed over her body, and that made the hum of music slink back into my head for a second, too. "I *knew* it."

"Yeah?"

"This place. After Dad bought it, I did a little research." She looked down for a minute. "Maybe I should've said something to you. I don't know why I didn't."

I didn't know, either. That wasn't like Jules, to keep something from me, you know? But I couldn't dwell so much on that, not if I wanted to listen. And I had a feeling that what she was trying to say was important.

"I think the house has a history. This area does anyway.

Some people say there was this hideout, like an Underground Railroad for witches, back in the Salem days. And there were drawings, illustrations of what the . . . um, I guess they were the safe rooms? Pictures of what those places looked like."

She took a deep breath. "They were lined in stone. Stones like that one. It makes sense. I had a feeling this place could be part of that story. Right location, and it's definitely old enough. I think Amity was one of those underground safe houses, once."

The tight, coffin-like feeling passed over me, even though it was broad daylight and we were standing in the kitchen, just as normal, as regular as could be. That sweet, rotten stink from the garbage can wafted by again, and for a second the entire room washed over red.

Then it was back to just me and Jules in the kitchen together, talking.

And the stone. My fingers were curled around it, pressing so hard the tips were bloodless white.

She was right again. I knew—I felt it, like a bug bite or a sting that you can't just slap away. The same way she was right about what happened to her down in the boathouse, the house kind of . . . working against her. And now, with the history, a little window on to what Amity truly was, always had been.

Jules was right.

THE FRONT DOOR CREAKED OPEN and Jules shot me a look. We both listened to the footsteps, so bone-tired and timid they could only be Mom's. She met us in the kitchen in her church outfit, a button-down flowered dress that had long sleeves and a skirt down to her ankles, even though it was sweltering today. Her cheeks were bright pink, but her eyes still had their usual flat, hollow look. She carried a battered-looking pocketbook made of fraying straw, and she sort of dropped it, heavy, onto the kitchen table, and sank into a chair right next to it.

"How was church?" Jules moved quick to pour Mom a glass of something cold from the fridge. She was always thoughtful that way, my sister.

"It was fine," Mom said, but her eyes stayed trained on the tabletop, like she was maybe holding something back. "Where's Abel?"

"He's upstairs napping," Jules said. "He, uh, hurt his hand. He's okay, just resting. And you don't look so fine." She slid a glass of ice water down, leaving a wet streak along the wood, which Mom rubbed with the sleeve of her dress. "You don't have a 'fine' face."

Mom smiled weakly. "No, it was nice, really." She took a long swallow from her water, then pressed the glass against her forehead, closing her eyes for a second. "I suppose . . . well,

I'd thought of asking if some of the ladies on the board wanted to come by for coffee," she clarified, getting to the point. "But there wasn't . . . a chance."

No one gave you the chance to ask is what I thought she meant.

She flicked her eyes across the room, over the peeled linoleum counters and the water stains on the ceiling. This fixer-upper wasn't exactly there yet. And Dad wasn't really big on unexpected guests.

"Maybe it's for the best," she admitted.

Jules nodded. "Maybe." She pulled out a chair of her own and sank into it, leaning forward on her elbows like she was getting ready to share a secret. "Have you . . . Did you talk to anyone about this place? The history here? Have you heard any stories about Amity? Connor found something—"

I stepped up behind Jules, real fast, and kicked at her chair leg. She pitched forward and made a face. After a minute, she waved a hand at me from under the tabletop, like she got it, she understood to shut up about the stone. If Mom hadn't seen it, hadn't noticed it, then maybe she wasn't supposed to.

"History?" Mom asked, like Jules was talking in a foreign language.

"There's a rumor, I mean. About the Salem witches. Hiding here."

Mom turned away, a sour look coming over her face. "Well, I never heard *that*," she said, kind of righteous.

She was lying. I don't know how I knew it, but she was. And she was lying badly.

"But you heard *something*, right?" I couldn't help it, couldn't stop myself from jumping in, gleeful and a little bit thrilled at the idea. "You heard *something* about this place?"

Mom heard the rumors. I heard the music. It drifted in now, from the riverbanks, slow and lazy, taking its time to get to me. Taking its time to whisper my name.

"There's *something* about this house, right? There is," I pressed, smiling.

Mom didn't answer. But she didn't need to.

Amity would answer me herself.

THAT NIGHT, I DREAMED, although what I saw—what revealed itself, I mean—felt less like a dream and more like a hallucination; some place that fell exactly halfway between what was really real, and what was . . . well, real to me.

I saw some place dangerous.

Dangerous, and inviting.

In the dream, I traveled, pulled by an invisible string, from my bed, to the basement, to the boathouse, and beyond, until I hovered, holding still, waiting to hear from her.

Waiting for Amity to speak to me.

I was over the river. Or in the river. Or maybe I *was* the river. Churning, angry and hungry and wild. Around me, on all sides, pale, bloated bodies thrashed and paddled, wide-eyed, panicked, pulling against the current. They were doomed, I could tell. But their energy fed my own.

My own, and Amity's.

We were melting together, becoming one. We were the same now.

She was a part of me.

When I lifted my hands from the river, they were washed in red, soaked in bloody stains.

Cold, clammy hands clamped down on my ankles, making me gasp, dragging me under the surface of the water, and now

I was actually bathed in blood, drowning-like, trying to breathe and gulping it in, tasting it like rusty metal in my throat.

Peeking through the ripples in the water, I realized: the fingers at my feet, tugging at me—they were shredded, strings of flesh and knobby bones and who knew how many years of decay. Some were witches', like Jules had said. But that wasn't Amity's only story. The boneyard beneath Amity was more than a specific place . . . wide and stuffed with bodies.

The fingers at my feet and the people all around me . . .

Who knew how long they'd been here, rotting, slowly dissolving into the Concord? Feeding Amity. And now feeding me.

I gagged. Shut my eyes. Let myself sink into the thick, sticky mud of the river's bottom.

She was a part of me, Amity. Growing, gaining power, every day. Amity wanted me.

And I welcomed her in.

NOW
DAY 8

GWEN

I WASN'T REMOTELY SLEEPY, and more than that, the images I'd come to see in my dreams lately had left me feeling . . . discomfited, to say the least. But my parents were worried, watching me; I could feel their gaze like

(a shotgun?)

twin drills trained at my back, more and more of the time now.

Pretending at normal became increasingly imperative for me.

The image from the bathroom mirror hadn't been back. But that didn't mean that her presence, heavy with threat, had gone. Not at all.

I needed to pretend at normal, so that night I changed into my pajamas as quickly as I could, loathing the creeping chill that passed over my bare skin like a breath from the beyond. I buttoned the flannel top all the way up under my chin, then turned my bedside lamp to its brightest setting. The glare made me squint, but I still preferred it to the alternative, the dim shadows that danced along the walls, taunting me, chipping away at my sanity.

Pretending at normal was easier said than done.

I wanted to say good night to my mother, to leave her with a sense that I was normal, happy, doing "well." I stepped into the hall, and my bedroom door swung shut behind me, banging like a clap of thunder and making me flinch.

Normal, Gwen. Normal. It was my momentary mantra.

I did not trust old houses, I decided. Or their histories. Histories were far too complicated, too potentially fraught. I had complications enough of my own.

I found my mother tucked in her bed, down comforter wedged beneath her chin, threatening to swallow her whole. She was leafing through a glossy, oversized design magazine, and I smiled bitterly to think anyone might successfully convert Amity, transform her, or reinvent her against her will. We couldn't keep the phone lines open, couldn't drive a nail into the wall, and lightbulbs never burned for longer than a day or two. Amity wasn't interested in ornamentation. She was no one's canvas.

"Gwen." My mother peered at me over the wire rims of her reading glasses. Her face glimmered with a heavy sheen of moisturizer, making her seem, in the purplish lighting of night, slightly hazy. Ghostly, even. "Going to bed?"

"Yes." I crossed the room to her side, bending over to kiss her on the forehead. Her night cream left a chemical aftertaste on my lips. "I was thinking . . ."

But *what* was I thinking? What alibi might keep my parents' hovering, their suffocating concerns, at bay?

"I was thinking that I might go into town tomorrow. Check out the local library."

Yes, that would work. Town: with people, public landmarks, and other fixed, immutable objects. In fact, why hadn't I ventured out before now? None of us had, really, beyond absolute necessity. It was almost as though Amity were emitting some sort of slow gravitational pull on us, as though Amity were *willing us* not to leave.

It was a *crazy* thought. *But nonetheless . . .*

"That's a good idea." My mother nodded, seeming satisfied.

Good. I had appeased her sufficiently. "Anything interesting in there?" I jutted my chin at her magazine.

"Oh, I don't know," Mom replied. "I had some thoughts about fixing up the boathouse. Making it into a proper workshop, or something like that. Luke was down there the other day, and he mentioned that the floorboards were beginning to rot. Apparently there's a huge storage locker in there, though, with all sorts of tools. Probably from the previous owners, but some of them look old. Murray chewed through a weak spot in the flooring, pulled up some old . . . well, *something*, maybe iron? So now Luke wants to dig, and see what else is down there."

I felt a by-now-familiar twinge in my palms. Reluctantly, I glanced down.

My hands, pink and raw, had sprouted blisters again, open and sore.

(*go away, crazy*)

I blinked, pressing the heels of my hands against my eyes, feeling the wet, weeping skin of the blisters on my cheeks, and when I looked up again, it was only my mother, her lips knit together in a thin line.

"Gwen?"

I forced the corners of my mouth up. *Normal, Gwen. Normal.* "Yes?"

"Are you . . . happy here?"

163

I swallowed, hard. *Normal, Gwen,* I reminded myself. *You have to be normal now.*

"Of course." I paused. "Aren't you?"

Of course, I'm happy. Of course, I'm normal. Of course, I'm not losing my mind.

Again.

"I am," she said finally. Her voice was clear, definitive.

But I could still hear the hitch, the waver, lurking underneath.

WITH MY MOTHER'S DOUBT REVERBERATING IN MY EARS, I traced a tentative path back to my bedroom.

Something in her tone—that tremor, that poorly concealed ripple of distrust—had worked its way into me, and now the hallway, which I knew by daylight to be a quick, straight path from point to point, now it yawned and stretched, so that my doorway beckoned as though calling from across a looming chasm.

And more than that, *worse*, more worrisome:

The door, which had swung shut behind me hard enough to rattle my teeth, was now slightly ajar.

And the light, which I'd so deliberately switched on?

The light was out.

From behind the gently swaying door, the room was utterly dark, utterly black.

The wiring, I thought, heart skittering frantically in my chest. *Fuses blow all the time here. They* do.

It was the truth. But it didn't make the darkness any more inviting.

I crept forward, one hand clapped over my mouth, forcing each footstep against the growing dread. Though the door continued to shift and twist, playing tricks on my mind, I reached it sooner than I expected, sooner than I would have liked. I stepped through the threshold of my bedroom.

The door snapped shut behind me.

I muffled the squeak that so desperately wanted to escape my lips. In the dark, I heard a scrabbling, a scrambling . . . the movement of some indefinable presence, defiling my space.

Well, that's the problem, Gwen. That you think of this as "your space" to begin with.

This space belonged to Amity, after all.

HEART HAMMERING and breath shallow, I edged my way along the floor to where I knew the nightstand stood. I fumbled in the inky dark, terrified.

The light flickered, casting a sickly glow over the space. I couldn't be sure, but I thought I caught the outline of a long slim leg, pale and mottled, escaping beneath my bed as the room brightened. Again, I swallowed back a scream. I shut my eyes tightly, and when I opened them again, the area beneath my bed was clear.

Whatever I imagined I had seen or heard had vanished.

But something else had appeared.

HOME, GWEN, YOU ARE HOME

I gaped, wide-eyed, at the mirror that hung from my closet door.

HOME, GWEN, YOU ARE HOME

It called to me in blocky scrawl, hand painted in jerky, frantic streaks of something thick and muddy.

(*home home* HOME)

The words covered my reflected face like graffiti, stark against my pallor, thrumming in my ears like a drumbeat, insistent and undeniable.

With a strangled cry, I raced through the joint bathroom and into Luke's room.

MURRAY GROWLED from the foot of Luke's bed as I rushed inside, blood pounding in my ears.

Luke was hunched over his desk, intent on something I couldn't see. He didn't stir until I grabbed for his shoulder.

"There's something," I gasped, "in my room."

Luke whirled around. His gaze was narrow, piercing. "What do you mean?" His pupils were slits, and I couldn't help but notice how sallow his skin was, in sharp contrast to the patchy stubble creeping up his jawline.

He looked tired, I realized. Drained. Like something was sucking the life out of him.

"I heard noises," I said. "And—there's something written on the mirror."

"You're nuts." His voice dripped with derision.

I bristled against his tone, his implication. Luke knew better, had always been kinder, than to say such things to me. Luke had always been the one to tolerate my intermittent madness. His dismissal now spurred me in a way I wouldn't have thought possible.

"Come look." I grabbed his wrist, dragging him back through the bathroom and into my room.

"See for yourself."

LEADING LUKE INTO MY BEDROOM WAS LIKE leading a rag doll. He wasn't protesting my guidance in any active way, only he seemed thoroughly uninterested, thoroughly absent from the entire experience. Murray followed reluctantly behind us, his ears flat against his head and his tail drooping in disapproval.

I paused in the bathroom, déjà vu washing over me like an unwelcome hug from a stranger.

The lights were out in my bedroom again. Before us, the space called like a deep, open wound.

"Congratulations, Gwen. You've really gone all out to create an ambience," Luke cracked flatly. "I'm not sure what I'm supposed to see in the pitch-dark, though."

Frustrated, I pulled him into the room, taking shuffling steps and trying my best to block out the slithering, scurrying noises that had—of course, *of course*—returned.

If Luke heard the scratching, crawling sounds himself, his body language gave nothing away.

A moment or two of flailing found the pull chain on the lamp again, which I tugged triumphantly. The lamp blinked on, and the room glowed butter-soft.

"*There.*" I pointed toward the mirror.

"*Where?*"

I looked up, following Luke's gaze, shrinking at the irritation in his voice.

The mirror was empty.

Clean.

The message—it was gone.

Murray, however, was whining, exhaling little whimpers and moans that built up steadily, increasing in intensity as he pawed at the gap beneath my bed skirt.

At the space where the streaky, ghostly leg had vanished just moments ago.

Luke kicked his leg out, connecting foot to dog rump. Murray squealed and fled the room.

"What are you doing?" I whispered hoarsely. Luke had never been anything but gentle with Murray, or any other creature.

He turned to me, his face blank, and put his hands on my shoulders.

"Gwen," he said gravely, "I won't tell Mom and Dad about this. But you have to . . . you have to get it together, you know? You can't unravel."

Again was the word that went unspoken. Always *again*.

His eyes bored into mine, blazing, and I turned from the heat, from the cut of them, craning my neck back to see our reflections in the mirror.

"I know," I mumbled, a choked sob cutting off as I took in the details framed before me.

There, in that mirror image, Luke's hands draped like talons over the tight points of my shoulders.

My stomach clenched.

Luke's hands.

Luke's *hands*.

In the mirror, Luke's hands were covered in dirt.

I FELT MYSELF SINK, panic flooding my body like a current. I trembled, and the bloody, gaping specter of my first night returned, rising up from behind me, from over my brother's shoulder. Her matted, clotted hair swung toward him, and I swallowed, steadying myself, but Luke remained motionless, even as the clumpy strands brushed against his cheek.

You have to get it together. The words echoed, ominous. I forced my breath, my heartbeat to an even pace, forced myself to look back at Luke, back at our entangled figures in the mirror.

His hands were clean now.

The bloody, broken being—whatever, *whoever* it was— was gone.

All that remained was my own tense expression, and next to me, Luke, solid and stern.

I pushed his arms away, stepped back against my bed.

"I'm fine now." I tried to keep the quiver from my voice, tried to sound convincing. "I'm . . .

"My mind was . . . playing tricks on me," I finished, hollow. "I'm sorry."

"It's okay," Luke said.

"It's nothing."

I wanted to believe him.

THAT NIGHT, I DREAMED, and the eyes through which my sleep-landscape unfolded, unfurled were not my own.

That night, I dreamed through Amity's eyes.

I *felt* her humming beneath my skin like a live wire. Felt her like a second skin, like a shadow draped across my shoulders, like a veil, a scrim, a silk-screened image of the past, the future, the beyond.

Amity was outside of me, pressing against me, choking me off. She was dark, heavy, and clouded with decay. She loomed, her shadow cloaked across the hilltop, something more than a place, more than a particular, specific space, more than beams, blueprints, boards, and bolts.

More than physical matter.

Amity surrounded me like a slipcase, slithering, stealthy, slick with potency. She breathed against my skin, whispering in a language not my own: wordless thoughts, formless shapes. Energy. Intent.

Evil.

Against my raging dreamscape, Amity's shuttered panes burst open, revealing all: everything of her before, her after. Her always.

Behind my tightly lidded eyes, Amity showed me:

(*an expanse of reddish, ruddy clay, rolling toward the river-*

174

bank, pebbled and marred and possibly diseased)

(soil and spoil and sour earth)

(a thicket of bramble, ghostly white and glowing, clattering like rolling bones)

(sickness)

(madness)

(fever and filth)

(runes and ruins, chalk-etched patterns and ink-thick pools of blood)

(fire and anger and sacrificed flesh)

Amity was the cold, steady gaze of a double-barreled shotgun, bearing down. She was the glint of pinprick pupils gleaming through a night-lit window, the rhythmic blast of a door left banging in a gale wind. The slither of a flesh-flayed limb beneath a bed skirt, a welcome note etched in blood. Amity's forever was reflected in the glimmering edge of an ax, in the rushing footprints, the twitching tail, the brushing fingerprints of a zephyr, a cipher, a wordless, formless shape.

That night, I dreamed, and in my dreams, Amity's shuttered panes burst open, shrieking and spiraling. Calling to me. Calling *for* me.

Foretelling. Forewarning. Foreseeing no hope of escape.

Amity called to me, insisting that I understand: her anger, her power. Her energy.

Everything.

Insisting that I see.

PART II

EVIL

FORM #3208A

STUDENT: Webb, Connor
GRADE/CLASS: 5th/L. Harper
EVALUATING COUNSELOR: R. Griggs, MSW

DETAILS: Evaluation requested by school offi-
cials after repeated disciplinary efforts failed to
have appreciable effect on the student. Webb's
record reflects consistent conflict with his fellow
classmates as well as school faculty and admin-
istration. Likewise, infractions have increased in
scale and intensity since first notation on record
(grade K), when Webb deliberately shut the bathroom door on a young girl's fingers, fracturing
two. (Explanation given: "She told me she was
real, but I didn't believe her. I wanted to see if
she would bleed.")

Though Webb is typically reserved (perhaps
pathologically so), his temper is quick to ignite.
When roused, he has repeatedly shown that he
will lash out physically and verbally if pressed.

Historically, he has great difficulty forming

connections with his peers; Webb's most note-worthy bond thus far has proven to be with his twin sister (Julianne Webb), more socially adept than her brother but demonstrating classic signs of enablement.

(*Recommend continued separation of respective class assignments to potentially offset unhealthy attachment. Teachers are also further discouraged from adopting or otherwise encouraging Webb's personal nickname for his sister, "Jules," who shall remain Julianne, or Annie, while enrolled in this institution.)

Formal evaluation requested after most recent incident: a quieter student (M. White) attracted Webb's attentions after the two were paired together for the school's annual science fair. Topic chosen by the team, as reported to Ms. Harper, was the relationship between sense of smell and sense of taste.

Project trials were conducted after school at the White residence; the boys' subsequent lack of supervision has been attributed to Mrs. White's work schedule.

Webb, who has acknowledged responsibility for conceiving and overseeing the project (despite White's protests), devised an experiment wherein White was blindfolded and given several substances to smell, ranging from the innocuous to the pungent to the noxious. White was then asked which substances he was willing to drink based on scent alone.

The next stage of the experiment involved blocking off White's nose (with cotton balls in the nostrils or a fabric sash tied around his head, White was unable to clarify) and charting his willingness to drink a second set of substances without the aid of sense of smell.

The second sample set contained only noxious substances. ER doctors were able to pinpoint three: laundry detergent, shampoo, and turpentine.

It is unclear to what extent White was coerced into ingesting the products; his teacher (Harper) reports that his desire for acceptance by, and approval of, his peers often leads to a complacent and easily suggestible personality. Regardless, when questioned in the emergency room after his stomach was pumped and his condition deemed stable, White insisted that he had been a willing participant in the experiment.

EMTs on site were able to determine that a 911 call had been placed from White's residence within 30 minutes of his ingesting the toxins. Webb was the caller; he was the only person at the house, other than White, when paramedics arrived. Medics described Webb's affect as "flat" and "detached," claiming that he seemed either unable to, or uninterested in, providing details necessary to aid their treatment of White. His responses to all questions were strictly cursory.

In my subsequent evaluation session with Webb, though reluctant to discuss the particulars of the science fair incident, he expressed coherence and awareness that his actions were "wrong," or unacceptable by external terms. He did not, however, convey any sense of guilt over the physical harm and mental anguish he had caused White and his mother. Webb is quick to disassociate from others' experiences, and shows acute, increasing difficulty in feeling empathy.

As the White incident represents an escalation in Webb's behavioral and social difficulties at school, it is my opinion that the boy is well on his way to demonstrating full-blown sociopathic tendencies. The only emotional reaction I witnessed from Webb was upon the arrival of his father to take him home; Mr. Webb's presence caused Webb to retreat, physically and emotionally. Though not confirmed in our session, this reaction suggests abusive behavior in the household that will surely exacerbate any antisocial tendencies in the boy, in addition to the obvious threat it poses to the entirety of the household.

Mr. and Mrs. Webb have ignored requests for a meeting or further sessions with Webb despite strong urgings.

It is recommended that a sharp eye be kept on the boy, that his teachers be made aware of his possible condition, and that he be required to undergo regular monthly evaluations, parental consent notwithstanding.

To the extent that constant adult supervision is possible given the typical student-teacher ratio, it is suggested that Connor Webb not be left unsupervised with others his age.

LAUREL VALLEY PSYCHIATRIC HOSPITAL
INTAKE PROCESSING FORM

Patient: Hall, Gwendolyn T.

Age: 12

Admitting Physician: R. Wood, MD/PhD

Preliminary Intake Details: Patient admitted at parents' mutual request. Presented at the time with mild hysteria (most likely trauma induced by the prospect of commitment, <u>not</u> official psychotic episode). Treated immediately with 4 mg Ativan and taken, restrained, to her room.

Consultation with parents revealed a history of mood swings, anxiety, and borderline delusional behavior, including the creation of elaborate narratives featuring a varied cast of imaginary friends. Hall has also presented with minor anger management issues, displaying a history of destructive, physical outbursts when agitated, which the patient insists are beyond her control. Parents determined to seek professional, in-patient care for Hall after a recent incident outside of school.

Hall attended a birthday party for a fellow class-mate, which her parents note is unusual in itself (the patient is a pathological introvert). The party was held at a classmate's home, and the children were engaged in a reportedly "typical" game of Truth or Dare. Hall, "dared" to retrieve an item from the base-ment, pushed another girl down the stairs.

Her reluctance to participate in the game evi-dently stemmed from fear of ghosts in the basement, which Hall claimed were speaking to her, "trying to get into the house. They needed to get in through me, and I didn't want to let them."

Hall's parents report that the patient insists it was "the ghosts," not she, who caused her classmate's fall, which resulted in a shattered patella. Hall her-self was unharmed physically at the time, though she has since lapsed in and out of consciousness, and her grasp on reality appears more tenuous than ever. Speech has regressed to the point of near muteness.

Also of note for her treatment is the fact that Hall's older brother, present at the time of intake, supports the patient's version of the event, agreeing that his sister did not push her classmate, claiming, "It was like with the stones. Just like the time with the stones." When pressed, he refused to clarify what he meant. Though not at the party, he believes his sister to be telling the truth. Mr. and Mrs. Hall assert no knowledge of the "stones" incident to which he refers.

Since the party (two weeks ago), Hall has not been well enough to return to school. Parents report that she alternates between near catatonia and extreme agitation. The family physician (A. Merrill) deemed the case beyond his scope and recommended treatment at Laurel Valley (*note reference form 46B, dated 11/2).

Preliminary diagnosis: Catatonic schizophrenia. Suggest possible treatment course (pending intake interview) consisting of (but not limited to):

individual counseling

group counseling

occupational therapy

electroconvulsive therapy (ECT)

medications:

benzodiazepines, mood stabilizers, antipsychotics

An Occultists' Guide to New England, 2nd ed.:
The Concord River Region, Part I]

(p. 86)

". . . though English settlement of the region in the early 1600s forced the dominant Memigassett population to Canada, it is believed that a small subsect of the tribe remained, mostly in hiding. Local folklore tells of the remnant tribe's discovery of stony underground terrain by the banks of the Concord River, bizarrely inconsistent with topographical maps of the area. They are rumored to have excavated improvised shelter within the stone outcroppings, (cave-like underground dwellings), despite a lack of recorded tools suitable for such masonry.

The survival of these tribesmen under such unfavorable conditions is often cited as evidence of their command of the black arts. Regional occultists specializing in shamanism claim to have unearthed bone fragments, artifacts, and other remains suggestive of Memigassett religious objects, leading to speculation that the cave dwellers used the surrounding area as

187

a burial ground for their magic makers and spiritual guides.

It has been argued, most recently by Bennett[47], that the ground itself where the tribe relocated was possessed of a great power or energy, and that the Memigassett who stayed behind channeled that power for their own purposes, appeasing whatever "original evil" lay dormant with the bodies—and the souls—of their own shamans. This theory certainly supports further reports of occult activity corresponding to the location of the underground stone caves. . . ."

(p. 103)

". . . Of course, the Wicca practitioners of the region either dispersed to safer areas, or went to great lengths to continue their practice in secret, leading to holes in our historic accounts of this period.

Many who were found guilty during the Salem Witch Trials did not, we understand, in fact possess any true magical powers, but this was not the case for all. Some, who perhaps saw the writing on the wall most keenly, are documented as having disappeared into a network of "safe houses" that cropped up intermittently along the westernmost stretch of the Concord River, the most widely accounted of which sat above a onetime Memigassett burial ground [see p. 86]. Letters collected from that area confirm the existence of this particularly well-trafficked stop on the "Salem Exodus" trail, though correspondence ceases abruptly in late 1693, with reference to a cave-in, possibly on, or nearby, the alleged burial grounds. . . ."

(p. 268)

". . . Graham Asylum, established in 1908, was one such institution, shut down in 1948 for unethical medical practices.

The more exhaustive of the contemporary occult scholars include Graham in modern lists of supernatural locales due to its geographic situation; verified area maps confirm that the original Eastern Wing rested directly above the "Salem Exodus" cave-in, believed itself to have been housed on Memigassett grounds. Blueprints show the "treatment room" as corresponding roughly to the Exodus hideout cave, leading to speculation[93] that an energy "hot spot," or nexus of negative power, might be said to originate (and, in fact, continue to reside) there. . . ."

TEN YEARS EARLIER
DAY 11

CONNOR

THE DREAM IS ALWAYS THE SAME NOW.

Always a nightmare.

And always the same.

Each night, Jules comes to me, her hair a bloody, blazing halo, flaming nuclear in the dark. She holds one finger to her lips and with the other, she points.

She shows—she *knows*—what needs to be done.

It's our father, she says.

He's the source of the danger in the house, in my blood. He's the reason for what I am, for what I've always been. *He* is the evil.

He must be destroyed.

I sit up straight. *"Destroyed?"*

But now that she's said the word out loud, I know she's right. I know it's the only choice, the way to free us all.

Also—and most important, I think—

I know it's what Amity wants.

Jules lowers herself onto the bed, the sheets leaking dark, clotted blood around her outline. She kisses me firm, her mouth against mine, her lips cold and slick. *You can possess it,* she says. *You can be the rage. Free us.*

You can own Amity, even as she owns you.

She guides me to my bedroom window. The moon glows through the splintered frames of the panes, lighting the Concord River.

I gag. The river runs red again, like it always does in these dreams—these *visions*, are what I think they are, really. It churns, dotted with gleaming stone chips that I think are bones, remains, decaying, diseased bodies, poisoning the water and the earth Amity was built on. The surface of the river bubbles, and my father's face appears in profile, damaged. Fractured. Ravaged.

In the dream, I know I'm the reason why.

I turn to Jules.

"I *will*." I swear it to her.

In the dream, Jules's body is whisper thin, traces of starlight peeking through her nightclothes. Her toes and lips are tinged blue-gray, and when she moves through the dream halls of the house, her feet don't touch the floor.

Jules guides us down the hallways, her eyes empty as she hovers at the cellar door. She holds a finger to her lips again, quiet again, as solid wood swings open, and we go down.

We're in the cellar then, but *past* the cellar, and deeper, sucked into the belly of Amity. We're on the other side of that stone wall, we've finally passed right through those enormous, round stones. Hunched in a hideaway, tucked up and sealed off, the earth-lined walls reek of vile, buried things. And even though I've never been here in my waking life, I recognize the space right away. I'd always recognize it, I think. It calls to me.

This is the red room.

Amity unrolls a reel of images to me, a bloody movie of her secret history:

A shriveled old man in a tall feather headdress. His face is lined with dark, oily war paint. He holds his arm up, shakes a stick at me.

I blink.

Not a stick, Jules says, her breath sticky and too sweet against my cheek.

I look again.

A human bone.

Bone. Crusted over with crumbling dirt that, I know by the tingle in the soles of my feet, lies right under me, right underneath the red room.

I reach to touch the bone, want to feel its muddy surface with my own fingers, and the image vanishes like a soap bubble.

This was a burial ground, I know. It was where the witches hid, and where the crazies were locked away. It was lots of things, and Amity shows me them all. But the truth is, this space—it's more than any of those stories. It's the rotted, black heart of Amity herself. I can feel that truth buzzing in my ears, ringing in my blood. The heart, the power of the red room—it was here before any of those specific moments, and it's been here ever since.

The red room will *always* be here. And right now it's here for *me*. Me and Amity, that is.

The movie unwinds: *These are the faces—the souls—that Amity's claimed.*

Their eyes droop. Their mouths gape. And somehow, I know them all. Witches, yeah. And inmates, sickos beyond help, tossed underground like garbage, chained up in this hidden cave to rot, if they were lucky.

Used for . . . other things, if they weren't.

The red room housed witches, yeah. And also sickos, crazies, and criminals . . . *And also others,* I think, watching a stray feather float past. Jules catches it in her palm, closes her fingers around it, and smiles at me.

They could channel the elements, Jules says. *They were here, even before Amity, and they claimed this land as their own.*

And when they died, their magic poisoned the ground below, right to its core.

"The red room." It's the core. And it was meant for me. I was meant to be here. I was meant to be with Amity.

In the dream, in this room, my father's true, *real* face appears. His eyes are blank, his skull fractured, crumbling away. Here, I can see, very clear—he's a demon. And he's filled with rage.

Jules floats up and out, beyond the house again. She rushes me outside, down the slope of our backyard. Her feet leave no marks in the damp grass as she delivers me to the boathouse.

The boathouse. There are things for me here, by the river. Things for here, where everything rotted and black washes to shore. *Real* things, even in this dreamscape. Gifts, from Amity.

A shotgun. An ax. A shovel.

Jules tells me—*Amity* tells me—I'll know exactly how to use them. I *will* use them. I have to.

And I *want* to.

In the dream, I see: my father is a demon. Boiling with anger. Shriveled as that old, poisoned shaman. It's the truth. But.

In the dream, I see: *me.* Amity. The red room, and all of its energy, rooted and reaching out. To me.

I have Amity. I *am* Amity.

And I know, completely, the truth that's always been, that's always *there*, sticking to me like a shadow:

The dream, the real, and the *real*-Real? There isn't any difference between those things. Not for me.

Amity has power. Dad is a demon. Jules must be saved. Those are truths, always, wherever I am.

And there's another truth, too, that I always carry with me:

Wherever I am?

I'm a demon, too.

NOW

GWEN

THE DREAM IS ALWAYS THE SAME NOW.

Always a nightmare.

Each night, after I close my eyes, horror overtakes me. It wants me. *Amity* wants me. And each night, when I close my eyes, she overtakes me like a gale force, showing me just exactly what she is.

In the dream, I am poised at the dock, the boathouse door banging a steady pulse. A thick, red haze coats the landscape, colors the Concord River a bloody rush.

I shudder, take a breath.

And dive.

Underwater, I open my eyes slowly to discover I'm not alone. The Concord is littered with bloated, pale bodies. They reach for me, these underwater phantoms, wrapping spongy, shriveled hands around me, pulling me beneath,

down, down, down,

and through, into the heart of Amity.

In the dream, a door swings open, revealing:

A secret space, not seen in my waking days. A shadowed, earth-lined room, shallow and dark as a coffin. Hard-packed walls laced with glowing, bone-white patterns that dance, hissing, whispering, singing to me. Showing me in flickering, flowing images, the true, wrenching history of Amity, of her poison, of her power.

This room was once a safe house, the specters murmur. *Once, it was a haven for conjurers, sorcerers, and other spirits, masters of the occult.*

Once.

Waterlogged fingertips brush at my ankles. I choke back a shriek and slap at my skin, my groping hands finding nothing but the pinpoint pricks of my own gooseflesh.

Once, too, it was a madhouse, an asylum for the diseased, the decaying. The ruined.

Do these voices surround me? Or are they whistling from within my own thorny, unreliable mind?

Somehow I know the answer is: both.

They were locked beneath the floorboards, behind the stone walls of Amity's cavernous cellar. They were forgotten . . . or worse.

A feather materializes, drifting slowly from the ceiling—*through the ceiling, how can that be?*—tousled by a breeze that doesn't reach my body, doesn't touch my skin. I open my hand to it and it settles, weightless, on my palm. Instantly, it melts away.

It leaves behind a watery, rust-colored stain that speaks to me of aged bloodstains and other dangerous things.

(*she was shot in the head*)

I wipe my hand against my hip and the voices return, somehow inside and outside my head in the same instant.

Once, this land, Amity's earthly terrain—once, it was a burial ground, where native spirits spoiled, sour souls seeped earthward, silent and potent, filled with unrest.

Beneath the house's baseboards, skeletal remains rattle, clatter, roll. I recognize them—they're the sounds I hear in my bedroom, in the early witching hours, and they are the figures that reveal themselves to me each night in my dreams. They slither from the walls of the

(*red room?*)

—yes, this room, the red room, the underground lair, creeping toward me, reeking of rot and filth.

The image from the mirror, the fractured girl, steps forward, emerges like a ghoulish beacon from the haze.

This is what he did to me, she says, her ruined skull glistening in the flickering light.

He'll do it to you.

I close my eyes, shrink in, contract, my heartbeat straining in my throat.

I blink, and I am back in the boathouse, a growing sense of dread creeping up my spine. Outside, creatures howl, mournful, louder than any known being.

The girl from the mirror is still here, suspended before me. Silently, she lifts a pale, translucent arm. She holds one index finger to her lips, and with the other, she points.

The boathouse is littered with boxes, with cases, with caddies and bins and baskets and buckets that rise, bursting through the floorboards, scattering clods of earth in their wake. They unclamp, slide open. She shows me:

A shotgun. An ax. A shovel.

The outline, the photo negative image of my brother—
of Luke—

his eyes alight, his lips drawn back. His head down, but still defiant.

She shows me:
Another outline, another image in negative tones.
A figure in profile—
ragged and ruined, jagged, fractured.
And dream or waking day,
within my mind or from deep beneath Amity:
The profile, I know, is my own.

BEFORE

CONNOR

THE TRUTH IS, the whole question of what to do about Dad started with Jules, way back when. She was the one who thought we'd be better off with him gone.

I mean, I agreed, of course, but she was the one to suggest it out loud, in real bald, bold terms. She was the one to say the thing we were both thinking—that twin thing again—out loud.

I remember the first time she brought it up. Remember it *clearly*, I mean.

It's not the kind of thing you forget.

We were little, still—young enough that talk like that could just be laughed off if the conversation got a little too specific for our comfort and stuff. Young enough that we could pretend to forget all about it after, if we decided that's what we wanted to do.

But, like I say—it's not the kind of thing you forget. *I* never forgot, and I'd bet money I don't have that Jules didn't, either.

Honestly, Jules was never the forgetting type.

We were ten, maybe eleven, even, but only just. Mom was pregnant with Abel at the time. I don't have to tell you, he wasn't exactly planned.

But, you know, shit happens, or so they say, and like it or not, Abel was on his way. Mom broke the news to us one drizzly afternoon, white knuckled and red eyed, while Jules rubbed her shoulder and I gnawed away on a hangnail. I personally didn't care much that there'd be a baby so much as I minded how it would affect all of us. It had been Jules and me for long enough, and we had a bond, you know, like a special twin thing, and it wasn't like we *needed* anyone else.

So as time went on, I wasn't too thrilled about the effect that the pregnancy was having on everybody; Dad raging from the minute he found out, and Mom, all typical, shrinking into herself so eventually she was just a huge, swollen belly and shoulders so slumped you wouldn't have thought she had a neck.

Or a spine.

Dad made it his mission to terrorize Mom day in and day out. Usually it was with the same old BS, but every now and then he'd come up with some new torture just for her. Like when he shut off the water valve, then beat her with a broken broom handle until she finally "confessed" how she forgot to pay the water bill.

If he hit her long enough, she'd own up to anything. And then he'd hit her for caving in, or for "lying" to him in the first place.

Even I thought it was twisted.

Jules and I, we got off easy with him. God knows he'd huff and puff, but he never laid a hand on us like he did Mom—and later, Abel. For us, there were never any major bruises.

I had some theories about why Dad left us alone.

ONE THEORY, IN PARTICULAR, that is, about why Dad mostly laid off Jules and me, why he mostly left the two of us alone: it was related to what the neighbors, the parents of the kids in school and stuff—what they thought about me, to why they kept anything they cared about locked up tight when they saw me come around.

The neighbors had enough suspicions, but Dad . . .

Well, there was that one time.

There was that time Dad caught me. Playing. With that cat. The first cat we ever had, I mean.

First and last.

Jules called him Flip, since that was what he did a lot of when he was still a kitten. But she didn't have too much of a chance to call him anything, because old Flip wasn't around for very long.

So, that one time, Dad was the one who found me. Playing. And that was better than if it were anyone else. Like, Jules would just have lost it completely if she'd been the one to come upon me, out back, with that cat. Even if she did always sense the truth about me, who I was.

Who I am.

Instead, it was Dad who turned the corner around the back of the old house, downstate. So he saw me, crouched behind the storm doors leading to the cellar, with Flip. I don't know if he really meant to sneak up on me, but I was pretty engrossed, you could say, in what I was doing when he crept up and over and got an eyeful. It just happened, like in a flash, and there wasn't anything I could do once he'd seen it. Everything was just completely out in the open then.

I was completely out in the open then.

And there was no going back.

I was young, but it must have been pretty clear what I was. What I *am*. Here was the proof.

Dad didn't say anything. Didn't even seem too surprised.

The apple doesn't fall far from the tree, after all. Isn't that what they always say? And I am one bad apple. Rotten. To the core.

There's probably a fancy doctor's term for it, some psycho–mumbo jumbo way to describe all the little chemical misfires in my brain that make me who I am. But, plainly put, it's this:

I am evil.

And I don't mind it at all.

BUT STILL, THOUGH, IT WAS *JULES* WHO FIRST HAD THE IDEA ABOUT DAD; getting rid of Dad *was Jules's* plan. From back when we were only *eleven*, when we were still kids, like I say.

I don't know, maybe I was rubbing off on her. They say that, too, after all: *one bad apple spoils the bunch.*

So maybe what was happening to Jules was she was being spoiled. By me.

WE USED TO HANG OUT IN THE ATTIC, in the old house.

Even back then I was basically a loner—parents weren't too encouraging about playdates, you know? But I could hang out with Jules. So we did, we hung out in the attic, even though it wasn't finished or anything, and there was this one dank, dusty section in the corner, like a crawl space under the eaves, where you could see the slats of the floor set all wide apart, and between them, cloudy, pinkish puffs of insulation. Mom told Jules that if you stepped in that section—if you just happened to put your foot down in *just* the right place—you'd fall right through to the second story of the house, just land smack in the middle of that upstairs bathroom, like randomly taking a shower had been your plan all along.

Neither of us totally believed her, but we weren't exactly taking turns stomping around that edge of the alcove or anything.

Nobody really cared what Jules and I did, what we were up to. Not even Mom.

Jules was playing with a lanyard, making one of those arts-and-crafts-y bracelets. It was a friendship bracelet, because, even though she was my twin, Jules still managed to have a friend or two from school. Still managed to be "normal," even with me for a brother. So Jules did things like weave friendship bracelets while we were up there, in the attic.

While I did things like play with the cat in my spare time. Like I explained. We each had our hobbies.

So it was quiet in the attic that day, which was normal for the two of us. I was flipping through a vintage Lovecraft comic. Nothing valuable—I wasn't some geek collector, just a fan—but I liked the pictures. So I was half reading, kind of, maybe more like skimming. The quiet was good for that.

"He hits her in the stomach," Jules said. She was matter-of-fact, not looking up from her lanyard. She spoke all casual, like she'd happened to stroll by a cool-looking shop window on her way home from school, and she just wanted to tell me about all the stuff she saw inside. But Jules was hardly ever casual, so I knew, right away-like, that something was up.

"Dad, you mean," I said. Who else could she possibly have been talking about? *Dad.* Dad, Dad, Dad. That's who.

"He hits her in the stomach. Or, at least, he did once. I saw it. After they thought we'd gone to sleep." She was still fixated on her bracelet, her fingers fluttering, knotting row after row.

"What, like, just out of nowhere?" Not that it would be too weird. Dad could go from zero to psychopath in the time it takes a person to drop their fork at the dinner table.

She nodded. "Well, they were fighting. So it's not like it was completely out of the blue. But I don't think Mom saw it coming."

"Mom never sees it coming." Well, she does, but she doesn't, you know?

"She was worried that he'd hurt the baby. But, I

think . . ." She tilted her head at me. "I think that was the *point*." She coughed.

Right.

"He's an asshole," I said. It was still a big word for me back then.

"Well, yeah." Jules got quiet again, studying her lanyard, turning it over and over in her palm. I wondered who the bracelet would be for when it was done—whether that person was someone who really *knew* Jules. Who knew our family's secrets.

Probably not. Jules was very careful about airing her dirty laundry. We all were. You sort of had to be.

Hell, I *was* her dirty laundry, lots of the time.

"We'd be better off without him." She spoke so soft I thought I'd imagined it. But the flush creeping up her neck told me I hadn't.

"Yup," I agreed.

I thought that was all there was to say on the subject, but then I heard another throat-clearing, flustered sound from Jules, and saw the flush on her neck flash like neon.

Like something toxic.

"We should just get rid of him," she said. "Just kill him in his sleep."

She said it clear, her voice loud enough that there was no mistaking her words. I knew she meant what she'd said.

I didn't answer right away. Not that I didn't see her point. The Webbs would have been better off without Dad around, sure, but more than that—the *world* could've stood to be rid of him, too. No question there.

But still: kill him in his sleep.

Kill him in his sleep.

The thing was, the playing around, the games and hobbies I had, they were messy, screwed up, for sure, but they weren't the same as killing a *person*. Not hardly.

Whatever was wrong with me—and I wasn't denying there was something wrong, never have, never would, never will—it wasn't *that* wrong.

Not yet.

What Jules was suggesting—it wasn't even too hard to imagine, honestly, the more and more I turned it over in my head, in that stuffy, dusty, cramped little space underneath the eaves. It wasn't too hard to picture. But what I'm getting at here, what I've been getting at all along, is:

It wasn't *my* idea.

That's important to remember.

It was Jules who suggested that things would be better for all of us with Dad out of the picture. We didn't act on it right away, or even talk about it again . . . until Amity.

But it was Jules who started it all, way back when.

No matter how things turned out in the end.

GWEN

THE STONES WERE JUST THE BEGINNING.

I didn't realize it at the time—I was ten, after all, and more than anything then, the stones felt like a twisted end-game of the tricks my mind had played on me for as long as I could remember. Stones raining from the sky in thunderous clumps, that's fairly apocalyptic material. So you can't blame me for doing what I could to put the memory out of my mind afterward, when it was all over.

Mom and Dad certainly didn't want to acknowledge it, wouldn't speak of it, disregarding any hints building to that day. I'm sure that's why we ended up moving after all, once it was over at last. *Truly* over, that is. After the hospital, and the treatments, and . . . everything. I think the hope was that relo-cation would be a fresh start, a clean slate, all of those brutally optimistic, fatally inadequate clichés about sunnier days ahead.

Thankfully, coming from a small town as we did, we man-aged to keep the story of the stones as small as possible. For my part—and especially after the treatments—I pushed aside any thought, any recollection, or even the stray moment of muscle memory—that called back to that buzzing sensation, roiling and building, under my skin.

Obviously, in light of what was to come, it wasn't an isolated incident, a random, freak occurrence.

In retrospect, what happened that day with the stones foretold everything that would come. After.

At Amity.

The time with the stones was a harbinger, a portentous manifestation of all of my damage. Even if the doctors—who also came later—would have termed that one of my classic *overreactions*. One of my signature moments of *hysteria*. Even if the doctors would have called it pure coincidence, I knew better.

I knew, even then:

The stones were just the beginning.

IT WAS A BRISK FALL DAY, the sort of late afternoon when the sky is streaked in vivid brushstrokes of color so full, so saturated that dusk itself takes on a three-dimensional quality.

Luke and I were in the backyard of the old house. I sat cross-legged on the patio, the cold of the flagstone seeping through the seat of my jeans. I was playing jacks, I remember; though the small metal pieces were elusive, and the process itself felt vaguely pointless—some grown-up's misguided idea of fun—the smooth bounce of the bright pink rubber ball against the pavement was satisfying.

The patio wrapped around the side of the house, and while I scooped up jacks halfheartedly, Luke practiced pitching a softball against the wall with maniacal zeal. He slammed the ball against a net he'd set up along the side of the house like he hoped to send it clean through the nylon. Sweaty and red-faced even in the afternoon chill, he stooped forward in an imitation of ball players he'd seen on TV. His attention was so pinpoint-precise, I abandoned all pretense at my own game.

Catch and release, catch and release . . . The hissing of the ball against the net was soothing, and I could see it was lulling Luke, almost hypnotizing him. It must have been doing the same to me, or I might have been more alert, more aware. Might have seen what was clearly to come.

As it was, we were both stunned when the reverberation built to a fever pitch, Luke pulling back, winding up, smashing the ball forward with the force of a tsunami. The net stretched back, and we turned, craning, and watched together as the ball sailed in a perfect arc over Luke's head. We were stunned momentarily, both taken by the powerful trajectory being traced against the sky.

We were stunned, that is, until we realized—both in the same instant, I think—exactly where the ball was headed. My eyes flew open as I met Luke's panicked gaze. At the sound of the ball shattering our neighbor's window, Luke winced.

"You'd better go inside, Gwen," he said darkly, shaking his head. "Before Sanderson comes out to tear my head off."

Old Man Sanderson lived next door, in a run-down split-level with enough peeling paint to render the house an entirely different shade from its original color, which had at one point (presumably) been a dusty blue. He was, as his name suggested, old in that bearded, balding, graying way. He was also not the sort of person you wanted to spend much time with under the best of circumstances, which these were certainly not.

"He's mean," I said to Luke, doubtful.

He *was* mean. Mean enough that neighborhood kids didn't even dare egg his house on Mischief Night. Mr. Sanderson was, we all suspected, the type of person to open his door to trick-or-treaters—after spiking a bushel of shiny red apples with fresh razor blades. He was the person around whom urban legends were built, a living, breathing cautionary tale for the children on our block.

"Exactly," Luke said. His gaze was hard, but I detected a telltale flicker of fear in the set of his mouth. "So go." He gestured again, emphatic. *"Go."*

I wish I could say I refused.

Nonetheless, I did manage to support Luke, without any conscious effort, after all.

Without any *conscious* effort.

I did still find a way to help my brother out.

ONLY SOMEWHAT RELUCTANTLY, I wandered inside, shuffling my feet along the ground. The relief I felt at being excused from the impending confrontation was offset by the guilt of leaving Luke outside to face Sanderson on his own. Our parents were out, off together on one weekend errand or another, and I couldn't decide if their absence made the situation better or worse. They would have been upset, of course, to know that Luke had broken a neighbor's window, but they would have known it was an accident. Luke wasn't, by nature, a troublemaker.

Not then.

And even back then, even before Amity, I was no stranger to hauntings. I believed, as everyone else did, that Sanderson was to be avoided at all costs.

I peered through the side window of the living room, nose pressed against the pane. Sanderson was making his way across our yard and toward my brother with a tight, grim expression on his face. His hair was thin and greasy, limp, streaked with more salt than pepper, and his posture was stooped. Everything about him curved forward, like the arc of a tidal wave, coiled and ominous.

Once Sanderson caught up to Luke, he began to shout. I couldn't hear what he was saying, but there was no mistaking the rising color in his cheeks, the furious pinwheeling of his arms. There was no mistaking the crease to Luke's forehead as he shrank back, drew in upon himself.

Through the window, I observed, transfixed, as Sanderson's gestures grew wilder, more menacing. He was irate, looming, expanding until he no longer resembled a wave so much as an exclamation point, a lightning bolt. Luke's eyes were round and glassy, and his mouth moved in mealy mumbles. He had progressed from panic to near terror, like an animal caught in a snare. I wished I could do something for him, something about that awful, sickening look. I couldn't imagine what, though.

I was only ten years old then, remember.

I couldn't imagine, but it seemed I wouldn't have to. Something was building in my core, in my center. From within, a prickling sensation bubbled and hitched, burning at the base of my throat, pressing at my rib cage urgently. And though it was the first time this feeling had arisen with such acuity, it was familiar somehow, still.

My skin felt tight, hot, itchy, as though my nerve endings were exposed wires, as though an electrical current coursed through me, setting me alight.

Then, suddenly, that shimmer, that charge, funneled out of me, streaking off into the atmosphere, leaving me dizzy, light-headed.

I rocked back with the force of all of the charged particles around me and in doing so, somehow solidified, pulling together, gathering whatever force was being built into a tightly knit ball that I could envision, just so, within my mind's eye.

From outside, I heard the low rumble of thunder, of air

pressure shifting, gathering energy. Our windows rattled and the sky darkened in a purple, bruise-like patch, collecting like a blood clot, swirling, coming to a vortex. Settling. Just above where Luke and Sanderson stood.

I blinked, trying to understand what I was seeing, why it seemed that whatever was happening, was only happening in my own backyard. I couldn't find a reason. But no matter; as it turned out, I didn't have time to dwell.

As it turned out, the stones were here.

THEY CAME ALL AT ONCE, in a pounding sheet, heavy and full, smacking against the flagstone and clicking like chattering teeth. The sound was crystallized, sharp, and bright, even through the windows, even from behind the safety of the living room walls.

As though it were coming from within my own mind.

Luke and Sanderson both stopped short, confusion etched on their faces. They tilted their heads up, shielding their eyes from the steady rain of pebbles, disbelieving. I wanted to shriek, to scream, to call out to them, to tell them—to *insist*—that it was ice, debris, anything that could be explained away.

Anything that didn't seem *crazy*.

But I couldn't bring myself to.

Because crazy or not, I knew: the rocks. Were *real*.

And they were mine.

LUKE DIDN'T SAY ANYTHING when he came back inside.

As the stones came down, I'd slithered along the living room wall into a crouch on the carpet, hugging my knees to my chest and biting down on my lip so hard I tasted the thin tang of blood. I heard the front door swing shut with a bang, heard Luke's footsteps, hard and heavy, moving with purpose toward the living room. I looked up at him as he crossed to the window above me, briefly resting a hand on my head. He frowned as he gazed out the window, alert and worried.

From outside, I heard a final, crashing boom, a clap, and a quick, heavy rain of pellets that sounded concentrated, thick. The stones had gathered, were rushing down with a final burst of force.

After another heartbeat or two, stillness fell, cool and lush. I felt it drape against my skin, velvety and dense, as much as I sensed it in the surrounding atmosphere.

The stones had come and gone.

My head felt clear now. All that remained was a dull throb, suggesting a hailstorm, a rain of something heavy and solid.

Suggesting the stones. Insisting that what had happened should not be dismissed.

Insisting that what had happened, happened because of me.

THE CALM, QUIET AIR WAS ALMOST as full, as pressing, as the stones had been.

"What happened?" I asked, my voice wavering.

Luke looked at me. "You tell me."

I swallowed. "I don't know what you mean."

But that wasn't quite true. Because this wasn't the first time, not exactly, that the laws of science, of physics, of gravity, of the typical movement of mass and energy—it wasn't *quite* the first time that these laws had rearranged themselves in my presence. It wasn't quite the first time that a prickle beneath my skin had gathered, bending the atmosphere around me, inverting it to my will.

Was it?

Now that the stones had gone and my breathing had slowed again, images began to replay themselves in my mind: fragmented moments, seemingly innocuous, easy to dismiss.

A glass vase tumbling from the mantel the instant my mother scolded me for playing in her jewelry case.

A pot boiling over on the burner as my parents' argument built to a fever pitch.

A lightbulb popping and burning out the moment Luke surprised me during an impromptu game of hide-and-seek, the charred, smoky smell lingering between us.

Fragmented moments, memories. Seemingly innocuous. Easy to dismiss. And so I had dismissed them. But between Luke and me, suspicion had always remained, suspended like a spiderweb, sticky and fragile as cotton candy.

Suspicion, and an unspoken agreement.

"I don't know." That was more honest. The stones were something new, something greater, and possibly un-ignorable. The stones were possibly too much for Luke and me to bear in secret.

Luke knelt down next to me, breathing hard. "Gwen—"

"What's it like out there?" I squeaked, cutting him off. My throat felt thick and rusty. Some inner warning bell was blaring now, telling me that whatever Luke was about to say might confirm our long-standing suspicion. Might bring it out into the open.

I wasn't ready for that.

Go away, crazy. The words danced in the air.

Luke made a hissing sound, sharp, through his teeth. "You'd almost never know. The only thing wrecked is *our* house. Our patio, I mean. And some . . . divots in the lawn, it looks like."

"But nowhere else." *Nowhere else.* I'd already known that, hadn't I?

"The stones only fell over our house, Gwen," Luke said.

The unspoken corollary hung between us:
Because that's where you wanted them to fall.

"Do you think anyone saw?" *And, if so, what will they think? What will they say?*

There were rumors and whispers enough as it was. Proof

of anything about me that went beyond "strange" or "fragile," anything beyond the rational realm . . .

Well, I guessed others wouldn't be so accepting of that. Those who'd never been privy to my flashes, my moments . . . they still weren't convinced that I was wholly normal.

Sane.

Luke shrugged. "Can't say. Nobody came outside. Nobody was looking out the window when I checked."

"Sanderson?"

"He was pretty spooked," Luke said. "I can't see him going out of his way to talk this up to people. What would he even say?"

Spooked. "Right." What would *we* say?

"So," Luke said, turning to me at last, his voice hardening with his expression, "I think this is probably something that we should try to keep to ourselves. As best as we can anyway."

I nodded, relieved. The warning bell calmed. Luke and I were coming to an agreement, then. I didn't understand what had happened, certainly couldn't explain it, so keeping it to ourselves made sense to me. I wouldn't even have known how to begin to describe what had taken place if I'd wanted to.

And I absolutely didn't want to.

ALWAYS

HERE

Here lies a plot of land, boundaries, borders bleeding outward, spilling soil, spoil, spreading a legacy of poison, a long, lethal history of bleak, black power; dangerous, venomous earth inching in every direction, seeding the landscape with danger, darkness, decay.

Here lies a collective of the forlorn, the forgotten, the forsaken. A tribe, taken, tormented, tortured. Left for dead and layered, levels deep, buried, bone against bone against bone.

Here lies the former site of a failed premise, a feigned promise, a pact as broken as the bodies that lay beneath, between, beyond. Here lies the hope of a haven, a safe house, a sacred space for magic users, shamans, and those who exist in the peripheral places of our world.

Here lies an in-between land, one which played host to a rotating, ever-evolving cast of struggling, searching hordes.

Here lies the legacy of ancient legends, lore long dismissed.
Force, power, soft and dormant. Dwelling silently, gathering,
funneling with the rage of a typhoon.

Here lies the apex, the access point to alternate planes, to
worlds beyond, to a forever of never and everything other and
dank.

Here lies Amity.
Now a house.
But always, ever,
 all unspeakable things.

Always awaiting.
Always amassing, absorbing,
reflecting sinister intent.
Always ready to snake its way under the flesh.
Always unsafe.
Not sane.

Always sentient.

Here lies Amity.
Always anger.
Always evil.
Alive.

Here lies Amity.
Always.

PART III

AMITY

NOW

DAY 13

GWEN

MOM BRIGHTENED when I mentioned to her that I was going to go into town, that I wanted to have a look at the local library. It had been several nights since we'd talked about it. She'd probably thought I'd forgotten, lost interest. It was important to my parents that my interest in "normal" social behavior not waver, so to her this development was good news.

She was sitting at the kitchen table, squinting through her reading glasses at the morning crossword puzzle. She asked hopefully whether I was planning on meeting anyone there, and I hated to have to remind her that I had no one to meet. The younger girl I'd spotted down by the riverbank hadn't come back—at least, not that I'd seen. And besides, I hadn't ventured from the property once since we'd moved in.

Which was odd, come to think of it.

"You can take my car," she offered, another sign that her concerns about me persisted. This type of generosity was uncommon, if not completely unheard of. Mom fished her keys out of a colorful glass bowl in the middle of the table and pressed them into my hand. The metal was cold against my palm.

"Sure." I wasn't going to turn down the car keys. If her concern reached a tipping point, it could be a while before I had my hands on them again. "I'll ask Luke if he wants to come."

Her shrug told me she expected this to be futile, and I had to agree. He'd been disappearing into the boathouse, shovel in hand, for longer and longer intervals lately, though he'd yet to show us anything he'd uncovered, promising only that it was "great stuff."

"*Great stuff . . .*" and that flat, distant gaze.

(*go away, crazy*)

I wondered what *great* meant in this context. I didn't think I wanted to know.

I slipped the car keys into my back pocket. "Do you need me to bring anything back?"

Mom looked startled by the question, then frowned. "No. I don't think there's anything I need. Oh, but, honey?" Mom's tone escalated, making my breath quicken. "If you're going to go get Luke, I don't think he's in the boathouse right now."

"No?" That was a surprise.

"He's in the basement."

The basement.

The basement, not the boathouse. A surprise, yes.

Whether it was an improvement remained to be seen.

THE BASEMENT SMELLED LIKE MILDEW, THICK AND CLOYING, making my nose prick as I tottered cautiously down the stairs. The only lighting was still that lone, bare bulb swinging from a fraying line at the foot of the staircase. As it arced back and forth, it cast bold geometric patterns in the air. I thought my mother had to be mistaken, that surely there was no way Luke would be down here in the dark, rank rot. Surely, this place was even less appealing than the dilapidated old boathouse.

(*not to Luke it's not*)

(*not to Amity*)

But as soon as my foot touched the cold concrete floor, I saw his shadow skitter along my peripheral vision.

He had a shovel in his hand.

Hearing me approach, he leaned it against the wall and pushed hanks of unwashed hair out of his eyes to survey me. I glanced around the spare, dreary room, finding no remnants of the sage I'd burned. Had Luke removed them?

And if so, why?

He looked at me, eyes flat. "You wanted something?"

I wanted lots of things, none of which I was going to get from my brother, my almost twin, in that moment. "I was about to go into town."

His eyebrows knit together in a suspicious question mark. "Why?"

Again, the question of why any of us would venture away from Amity. It was a valid one. Until now none of us really had left, more than we needed to.

I ran the toe of my sneaker along the basement floor. "Actually, I wanted to check out the library. I'm interested in local history." Mostly, I was interested in seeing how the public records might correspond with the garish dreamscapes I'd been encountering lately. "I mean, specifically, the history of the house. It's got such old bones." *Old bones.* The skittering from my bedroom, from within my walls at night, sounded softly in some far-off corner of my mind.

(*go away, crazy*)

I went on, babbling a bit now. "You should know. I mean, all that poking around you're doing in the boathouse. You must be getting pretty familiar with Amity's bones." A whisper of cold air rushed over my bare arms, making me shudder.

Luke jutted his lower lip out. "And where," he sneered, "do you think that's going to get you?"

I'd expected this anger, hadn't I? Luke defaulted to it more and more these days. As calmly as possible, I replied, "I'm just curious."

Of course, they say that curiosity killed the cat.

Luke's face relaxed slightly. "I don't think you'll find anything."

That skittering again from the back of my throat, fluttery movements in the corner of my eyes. *Go. Away. Crazy.* I swallowed.

Luke flicked his eyes toward a lightless, sooty corner of the room. Following his gaze, I caught sight—just barely—of a torn, dingy plastic bag, lumpy and leaking a small pool of dark fluid. My stomach lurched.

"The thing is, Gwen," Luke said, his consonants long and drawn out, "I kind of know everything I need to know about this place already."

I decided I wasn't interested in any further details from my brother.

(*What's in the bag, Luke?*)

(*she was shot in the HEAD*)

I told him I'd leave him to it. And I did.

MY MOTHER'S CAR HAD SEEN BETTER DAYS, but pulling down Amity's long, winding drive and out onto the pebble-strewn road felt exhilarating. I rumbled along with the window rolled down and my arm resting over the door, baking in the sunlight as the breeze whipped my hair against my face. But I'd only gone a mile, maybe, when the sky clouded over, gray swaths of steel wool connecting overhead ominously.

I hardly had time to register the swift shift in weather when a fawn bounded out from the wooded thicket that lined either side of the road. In a single leap, it jumped to the center of the road, velvet-lined nose twitching. Its chocolate eyes bored into mine as the car chugged forward, seemingly of its own volition.

I gasped, squeezing my eyes shut involuntarily, bracing for the impact. But there was none.

When I opened my eyes again, the deer was gone.

But the figure from my bathroom mirror had taken its place.

SHE WAS THERE IN A HEARTBEAT, a hairsbreadth, a flash, a tangle of dark, matted curls slapping my windshield and fanning out. There was the thud, the groaning protest of metal against muscle, the slam-rattle of glass against bone, my teeth clicking together as my own head snapped forward in my seat.

She was holding something in her hands, holding it out to me, even as her limbs pinwheeled at odd, impossible angles. I glimpsed stained—was that *fur*? Was it felt or fabric? It was too quick, tumbling away—and then reflexes overtook me.

I jerked the steering wheel to the left, sending the car screeching into the drop-off that sloped alongside the road. The car stalled out, flinging me harshly against my shoulder harness. I quickly unclipped it and stepped out of the car, panting. I climbed back up out of the ditch and onto the road, coughing from the smoke rising from the hood of the car like fog.

Even through the haze, I could see there was no trace of the girl, not a hint left behind.

BACK UP ON THE ROAD, with an elevated vantage point, the situation with the car looked all the more dire. I had nothing but the car keys in my pocket, so walking home looked to be the only option. I was alone on the road,

It was lucky, I supposed, that I hadn't made it further into town.

"WHAT HAPPENED?"

I whirled to find myself face-to-face with the girl from the sewing room window, the one who had disappeared down by the river. The canopy of the woods behind her remained completely motionless, undisturbed.

She was waiting for my reply.

"I thought I—I thought I hit something," I said, those glazed, red-rimmed eyes, that matted, clotted nest of hair, that ghoulish image from the mirror streaking through my mind. "A deer."

There *had* been a deer, hadn't there?

"You *did*. Hit something." She pointed, and I followed her gaze.

There, on the windshield, where the mirror-image had made contact with my car, crept a nasty spiderweb of cracks. In the center, an angry red smear screamed accusingly, a bloody target.

The air around me seemed to fall away. "But . . . ," I faltered.

Knowing seeped from her, leaked from her sea-green eyes. "If it *was* a deer, then where is it?"

"I don't know. The impact, maybe?" I scanned the shoulder for any trace of an injured animal.

There. The dirty felt—that stained, furry fabric. The one that the figure had held out to me. It was lodged under one of the car's front tires.

That much, at least, I hadn't imagined.

"That," I said, gesturing toward it. "What's that?"

She hitched up her pants, faded jeans that sagged in the seat, and darted toward it.

"Oh, you shouldn't—" I called out, worried that it was maybe a wild animal, broken and battered beyond saving. I hadn't meant for her to try to get a closer look. But she'd already snatched it up and was making her way back to me, clutching it against her chest.

It *was* an animal, I realized, as she drew closer. But not a live one. She was holding a small, stuffed dog.

It was covered in bloodstains.

The stains had streaked across her top, a loose, cotton piece that had been cornflower blue to begin with, but now appeared a wild, modern-art print, dusted with handfuls of road grime and smears of . . . yes, it was definitely blood.

I swooned.

"YOU SHOULD PUT THAT DOWN," I managed, when the wave of dizziness finally passed. "It's filthy." And we still hadn't found the presumably injured deer. *And* if the object that the mirror-image carried was here, then where had she gone?

(Go. Away. CRAZY.)

None of this made any sense.

I swayed again in the heat, knees buckling as the air in front of me appeared to ripple, to shimmer and bend.

I felt the girl's hand on my forearm, cooler to the touch than I would have imagined. "It's okay," she assured me. "It's mine." She meant the stuffed animal.

I looked down at her, searched the toffee-colored freckles splashed across the bridge of her nose. "It's *yours?*" This, too, made no sense to me.

She shrugged.

A SURGE PASSED OVER ME, slinking along my skin. There was a sharp clap of thunder overhead and I flinched, bracing for a deluge, but none came. In the distance, lightning forked neon through the sky.

"I'm Gwen," I told her. "I saw you down by the river."

"I know," she replied. "I'm Annie."

"That's a nice name." Though it didn't quite suit her, even with her moppish, live-wire ponytail of copper curls, and those round, baleful eyes.

"It's babyish," she protested. "It's not . . . *me.*" She pursed her lips and again, that charge ran through me. Again, thunder echoed, rumbling, from all sides.

I focused on a brownish-red stain at her breastbone. It looked like a half-moon, blooming just above her heart. Looking at it, I had to shudder.

"So what would you prefer?" I asked her. "What is *you,* then?" I tried to tease, to speak lightly, but my voice rose, reverberating in the humid air like a tuning fork.

"Don't worry." Those baleful eyes narrowed.

"You'll find out."

THE GROUND RUMBLED before I had a chance to respond to Annie. Hearing the low growl of an engine, I turned to find a boxy, bright yellow hatchback moving smoothly toward us.

The car pulled up so that the driver and I were parallel. It was a woman with muddy brown eyes and a severe middle part in her dark, shoulder-length hair. She kept her hand on the gearshift as she regarded me.

"Need a ride?" she asked.

I did, obviously, but still wasn't used to small-town life and didn't fully trust a stranger's intentions. A shortcoming of my own, maybe. But also, there was Annie to consider.

"I'm okay, actually," I insisted, smiling in a way I hoped appeared confident. "I'm not far from home. I guess that's the good news." I gestured down the road, back from where I'd come, where Amity stood, isolated and apart from the fabric of Concord. "We just bought—"

She grunted, cutting me off. "Oh. You're the ones who bought Amity." She frowned. "How're you finding it?"

"We—" I considered. "We like it. I was just trying to get to the library, actually. To see if there was any information about the house's history."

She scowled. "Well, you wouldn't've found anything

anyway. There was a flood a few years back. Concord River rose during the rainy season. Water got all up in the library, through from the basement and halfway up the ground floor. Records were all destroyed."

It felt like a punch to my stomach. "Oh." The word came out slowly. And what had Luke said earlier? That he already knew what there was to know about Amity? "Well, then, I guess it doesn't matter that I won't be making it into town today."

"I guess not." She clutched at the gearshift, manipulating it so that the car bucked, the engine snarling. "I'll call for a tow for you when I get where I'm going. But you should be getting back to the house now. Sooner than later, you know?"

I forced a smile as if her words were light, innocent. As if she weren't hinting, I suspected, at something more. As if I weren't certain that I felt, that I sensed, Amity's tug on me even now, even as I stood here, stranded on a backcountry road.

She didn't smile back. My own grin faded and my hands fell to my sides.

She coughed, and sped off into the distance.

"ANNIE. ARE PEOPLE AROUND HERE ALWAYS so unfr—"

I paused, my stomach a trapdoor that had just been released, my throat dry, tight, closing fast. Around me, the woods seemed to hold its collective breath, the air heavy with moisture, roiling with the threat of a storm.

Annie was gone.

She had vanished. Her doll, her sad, stained stuffed dog—it had disappeared with her. And that wasn't all.

The bloody strike, the nest of shattered glass spread across the windshield of my mother's car?

Both of those had vanished, completely, as well.

TEN YEARS EARLIER

DAY 15

CONNOR

3:14 A.M.

I felt a tug, like clammy fingertips, at my toes.

Go away, I thought, though I couldn't've said who I was talking to. I kicked my feet and rolled over. That's when I realized:

The ground was hard, solid underneath me. Instead of my mattress, or a sweaty mess of sheets and blankets, I was pressed against wood, all knotty and warped against my bare chest.

It was like . . . like waking up inside of a pine box.

I snapped my eyes open. *"Where—"*

I realized right away.

The boathouse.

I could hear the slosh of the river lapping against the dock posts, could smell the algae creeping along, slick and slimy against the bottom of the rickety little shed.

Somehow, I woke up in the boathouse.

There was a shovel next to me.

Someone—or some*thing*—wanted me to dig.

Amity, I thought.

I stood.

THE NEXT MORNING, I WAS BACK IN MY OWN BED.

When I opened my eyes, I thought I remembered, sort of, the boathouse, the shovel. And digging, maybe? Did I dig last night?

The sun was bright, really pounding through the window, shouting at me to get moving. I tore the sheets and blankets off and threw them on the ground. My spine crackled when I swung around and lowered my legs onto the floor. I was coughing the last dregs of night up when my eyes finally focused and I caught sight of my feet.

They were covered in mud.

Next to the bed there was a battered old binder, filthy white plastic that was cracked at the corners. It was covered in mud, too. It stank like the air in the boathouse, like that dead-body rot I smelled in my dreams.

Did I dig this up? I couldn't say. The buzzing in my fingers made me think yes.

Was this what Amity left for me in the boathouse?

I grabbed the binder and flipped it open. It felt like being electrocuted, kind of, when my fingers touched the cover. But in a good way. It was some kind of scrapbook, filled in with hole-punched newspaper articles and other clips, some pages like a photo album with the clear sheet over the sticky stuff.

I turned the pages, skimmed along. Some of the clips had highlighted parts. *Memigassett*, I read. *Burial rituals. Nexus of power.* It was like reading along to the pictures I'd seen in my dreams.

There must've been a breeze then, even though I didn't feel it, because the pages kind of ruffled on their own. On my lap, the book flopped open to a bold headline, like almost a scream: **THE CONCORD RUNS RED AGAIN: FAMILY SLAUGHTERED AT AMITY.**

The date on the article was the future. But close, like something that was going to happen real soon. And there was a picture, too. It was blurry, hard to make out, but I could tell:

It was a picture of me.

I didn't bother to wonder about who put the book together, or why it was important to get it to me, or even how there was a newspaper clipping from a date that hadn't happened yet. None of that stuff really mattered.

It was pretty cool to see my picture there, honestly. Even all blurry.

I liked it a lot.

THERE WAS OTHER STUFF IN THE SCRAPBOOK, TOO, like information, I mean, about Amity. And, yeah, it was all pretty similar to what Jules told me at night, in those waking-dream times.

I read this thing about the basement, which I'd kind of already guessed. Those giant, smooth stones were used for walling up hideouts, like all way back when. So later that day, I went down there, into that stale dark, tapping along the walls, listening for echoes, wondering what was buried on the other side. Nothing knocked back. But I was listening, ready.

I remembered about the red room from my dreams, you know? In the dreams, I'd been inside of it, like right in the middle of all of Amity's strength. I wanted to get back in there, to be in there all of the time, as much as I could.

So there I was, tapping along the wall, banging my knuckles all over, listening for hollow places. The stones looked smooth enough, but they were scratching up the backs of my hands pretty good, and actually, it kind of sounded like *all* of them were a little bit hollow, were echoing, like kind of calling out, you know?

I crouched, knees popping. Right under the staircase, the basement floor was poured concrete, but as I ran my hands along the ground, my fingers grazed the little space where the wall and the floor came together. Right there, like a little skinny gutter, sort of, where the concrete stopped, I could feel cold, hard-packed dirt. I pressed at it and it gave, just a little.

Interesting.

You couldn't dig up concrete, not without serious equipment.

But you could dig up the dirt.

And I had myself a shovel, right? As of last night. It was right outside, in the boathouse. It was waiting for me there when I woke up in the middle of the night. It was *still* waiting for me there.

I just needed to go and get it.

THE SHOVEL *WAS* THERE, propped against the door to the boathouse, just resting upright, like it knew I'd be coming to find it, to use it, today. Like it knew I went down to the basement and saw something that was maybe worth digging up.

I picked up the shovel. The rusty metal of its handle was rough.

"Connor."

I almost jumped. For a minute there, I kind of forgot about the rest of the world, you know? Like everything just fell away, except Amity. But here was Jules, coming up behind me, clapping a palm on my shoulder.

"Jesus." I shook her off.

She moved back a few paces, eyeing me kind of funny. "What are you *doing* out here?" Her voice squeaked.

"Nothing." Why was she so bent out of shape anyway? "I wanted the shovel."

"Clearly." She twisted her hair in a knot at her neck. It was still wet from her morning shower and the shoulders of her T-shirt were soaked. "You left a mud pit in the bathroom this morning."

"Sorry," I said. I tried to be nice about it. But I wasn't sorry, really. Mostly, I wished she'd leave me alone. I wanted to be by myself, didn't want Jules poking around in the boathouse right now. Not for any reason, I mean. It just was.

"Getting into trouble out here?" She said it kind of joking, but I knew Jules well enough to tell it was a serious question.

"Come on. I just got out here," I said, even though we both knew I never needed too much time to get into trouble. I could find trouble on a dime. Usually did.

Jules shot me a look. "You were using that shovel for *something*," she said. She pointed her finger right at the same time as her jaw dropped down to her knees. "Connor. What the *hell*?"

I looked where she was pointing. It was the tip of the shovel, all crusted over.

Streaked with gore.

Interesting.

A head rush came over me and I rolled my shoulders back.

"What were you digging?" she asked. Her voice was all hoarse and raspy.

I stared hard at the shovel, trying to tell myself that the reddish clumps at its tip were just rust, or clay from the riverbank, or something. But inside my head, even through all of that static and fuzz, I knew better. I knew the truth. Even without being able to remember too clear.

It's blood.

My eyes closed, that charged, rushing feeling coming back over my skin. My mouth wanted to pull into a grin.

Interesting.

Rather than tell Jules that I had no idea, frankly, what I'd dug up, I thought I'd see for myself. I shoved her out of the way and tossed the shovel down so that it landed flat on the ground, spraying some pinkish-white gunk up as it fell.

I threw the boathouse door open and went in.

JULES WAS RIGHT BEHIND ME, so once we got inside, she was the one who saw it first.

My eyes flew from corner to corner all quick, but not really taking any of it in. It was the same old boathouse as always, stinking like mildew and pond scum, with wet sections of wood curling up in splintering hunks. The floor was rotting away, and mud bubbled up through the holey parts.

I was thinking, *You could dig there. You could dig all of that mud up if you wanted to.* I still didn't remember doing that, but I was caught up in thinking about it when Jules saw what she saw, and screamed.

Her shriek was sharp like broken glass, right in my ear. It made my teeth go all on edge, and for a second, I felt like I wanted to hit her. Or worse.

"*Connor,*" she sobbed. "What did you *do*?"

She grabbed me, really pinching my arms, and swung me to the left corner of the shed. She was so upset she was hyperventilating, sort of, digging into my skin with her gnawed-up fingernails.

There. There it was. There *they* were.

Squirrels. A little family, looked like. A mama squirrel and three little babies, curled tight, real still, piled up in a nest of leaves.

253

It would've been kind of cute, I guess, if it wasn't for all of the blood.

Whatever killed the squirrels just completely ripped them apart. Mama's torso was split from right underneath her chin all down between her rear legs, a mess of oozing innards pouring out. The babies' heads were twisted so far around they were looking over their shoulders. Their paws were caught up in Mama's guts and the nest leaves were all shredded and stained with blood. A little cloud of gnats hovered over them. It was pretty gruesome.

I smiled.

Jules let go of my arms. Behind me, I heard her retch. "What the hell?" she asked again, her voice kind of choked.

That static was back, a hornets' nest in my head. "I didn't—" I stopped.

I didn't do this was on the tip of my tongue, just a reflex, really, but the truth was . . .

I couldn't remember.

Maybe I did.

"I'm going to be sick." Jules moaned, running out the back of the boathouse to the edge of the dock and leaning over just in time. She dropped down to her knees and spewed for real this time, shoulders heaving all up.

I heard a bang. *The shotgun,* I thought, and then realized— *of course*—the boathouse door just slammed shut behind us. *Of course, of course. Amity.*

I heard a cracking sound. It was the dock, and the snap it made when it split in two was way brighter, louder, than you would've expected that old, soggy wood could make.

There was another scream. It took me a minute to get that it was Jules again, louder even than when she saw the squirrels.

I watched as she plunged from the dock into the water and down.

EVEN HEARING JULES HIT THE WATER, for a second there, I was still mostly interested in the squirrels. Wondering what happened to them, I mean. Whether *I* happened to them.

It's not like it would've been the first time, you know?

So I was kind of caught up for a second or two, like not paying attention so much to my sister. But then there was that sharp, snapping sound, and that cut-off shriek, and then a splash, and I understood that the river, she had Jules.

Which was maybe the one thing that could have pulled me back, away from the squirrels.

I rushed out the back door onto the dock. I could see the jagged edge of plank where the dock broke off, where Jules fell. I dropped down, just like Jules had, and saw her flailing, hair coming loose and fanning out all around, right under the surface of the water. She tilted her head back and just broke the surface, but when she opened her mouth to call to me, the river rushed in, choking her off. She sputtered, slapping her arms up and down again, her eyes getting wide and nervous.

She could swim, but just barely. It was the same with me.

The shovel, I thought, and ran back for it.

I HELD IT OUT TO HER, AND JULES GRABBED AT IT, desperate. She caught the slime-streaked blade and wrapped her hands around it. She kicked and coughed and I pulled, throwing my whole body into it.

Jules squawked my name once, twice, then disappeared under again, her fingers pressing hard into the metal, turning white.

There was a pull on the other end of the shovel, like someone had Jules by the legs and wasn't going to let her back up on the dock, back up to me.

Amity. I could feel her power in the air all around us. The static in my head was louder now and, for a minute, I thought about just letting go—just leaving the shovel to sink, and Jules along with it.

For whatever reason, Amity wanted her gone. I thought that was enough for me.

I uncurled my fingers and let the shovel go a little bit slack.

With one hand, Jules slapped at the water, fingers waving panicky now, bubbles rising from where her hair streamed out like a big, gaping wound.

Jules. This was *Jules* in the water, underwater, drowning. The one thing—*person*, I reminded myself, *person*, not *thing*—I couldn't let Amity take.

I grunted, trying to concentrate and push through that buzz, bracing myself. I slid forward as far as I could, thinking I was for sure following Jules into the water any minute.

Of course, if I did, whatever was wrapped around her legs would welcome me. Would help me back to shore. What Amity wanted from me was different.

Maybe there was a reason Jules was being held under, being held back, you know? Like a good *reason* Amity wanted her, in that different way, I mean. Wanted to destroy her.

That buzz inside, it burned at me, saying maybe Jules was *supposed* to stay under, was supposed to be buried. Supposed to be part of the Concord, of Amity, that way.

Her fingers twitched against the shovel and I blinked. A bottle rocket exploded in my temples.

I shook my head and opened my eyes, breathing hard.

Jules.

This was *Jules*. In the water. The one thing—*person!*—I couldn't let Amity take.

I flexed my elbows, yanking her back with all of my strength, everything I had in me.

HER ARMS BROKE THE SURFACE FIRST, white as bone, and then her face, turned up to the sky and gasping huge swallows of air. Her T-shirt clung and her shorts were soaked, sagging low as I pulled her over the edge of the dock. Once we were safe—steady, I mean—she flopped over, barely looking me in the eye.

She looked worn-out. Dead, almost, like something dragged back from beyond. The sun disappeared behind a cloud, and I thought, again, how maybe she was *meant* to be drowned. That buzz sparked behind my ears, the corners of my mouth wanting to jerk up again, wanting to grin.

She coughed. "Something was pulling on me," she said. "Something was keeping me under there." Her voice was flat.

"Come on." I gave her my most blank, most not-real face. I didn't usually do that with Jules, but the static, it was pounding now. It felt like that blank look was all I could handle. "That's nuts. Like what?"

Her face tensed like she knew I was bullshitting her. "You didn't come after me. Not right away."

I couldn't think of what to say to that. I mean, I pulled her up, right? Eventually? I didn't let Amity take her.

After a second, Jules started to cry, big heaving sobs that made her whole body shake. "You didn't come after me," she mumbled again, her voice thick.

Usually Jules's crying just breaks me in half. But right now anger flared red behind my eyes. I pulled her back up finally. Even though Amity wanted her. And here she was, still whining.

I hated her for a moment.

I was thinking I should have maybe let her go.

Ignoring her sniveling, I picked up the shovel and walked back up the hill to the house.

Back to Amity.

DAY 16

GWEN

LUKE HAD TAKEN to sleeping in the basement.

By our third week at Amity, this had become his regular practice. Mom and Dad didn't comment on it—at least, not to me. I was too fragile for their nervous speculations, of course.

I had my own opinions on the phenomenon, nonetheless.

It seemed an odd choice, given how dank the basement was, smelling like mold and sharp, overripe mildew. But Luke insisted it was the only place in the house that ever felt warm at night, and that point was hard to argue.

I had resigned myself to involuntarily waking at 3:14 most mornings, regardless of how soundly I was—or wasn't—sleeping. I wondered whether Luke dreamed of shotguns, too.

He was sleeping later and later, and after a few nights of his basement hibernations, my curiosity

(killed the cat)

overrode my unpleasant suspicions about the basement, about what it contained, and how it might be working its will on my brother.

Working its will, Gwen? Its will?

Don't be

(insane)

silly.

It was a *room*. In a *house*. It couldn't *feel*, couldn't *emote*, and it certainly couldn't commune with the living. It had no will to speak of. Houses did not work that way.

But what about the waking dreams? my inner voice persisted, pressing. *What about the images, the slow, languid, abstract reveals of Amity's history? Of her power?*

What about the red room?

If my waking dreams held any truth, this "red room" existed. It had strength. And it was underground, tucked within the walls, just behind my brother's makeshift bedroom.

IT WAS AFTER LUNCHTIME when I found myself at the entrance to the cellar, wavering. Luke had brushed past me an hour earlier, unwashed, hair uncombed, his clothing wrinkled and strewn with lint, muttering something about firewood. A saggy plastic garbage bag like the one I'd seen in the cellar the other day was slung carelessly over his shoulder.

Did we *need* more firewood?

Maybe.

Or maybe . . . *maybe* . . . Luke *needed* more time with the ax.

Like so many other unbidden thoughts, I pushed the idea as far from my mind as I could. I had grown more adept at doing so since arriving at Amity.

I'd had to learn, to adapt—in order to stay

(*alive*)

sane.

THE CELLAR DOOR CREAKED as I pushed it open, the sound like a yawn, a stirring. I felt small, vulnerable as I ventured downstairs.

Luke had set a few rusted table lamps strategically along the walls. In the orange-tinted light, I could see more vividly the boxes we'd stowed here, those containing our least essential belongings. There was nothing appealing about venturing further downstairs. To me, basements were shadowy spaces of containment, concealment. And I've always had enough shadowy spaces of my own.

But there was the curiosity.

The first thing to hit me as I descended was the smell: acrid, watery, like a carpet of moss. Luke was right about one thing: it *was* warmer down here; through the walls I could hear the occasional whirring of machinery as the boiler and other piping chugged away.

But the warmth and the odor together formed something beyond the sum of their parts. Stepping into the basement was like stepping into a swampland on solid ground.

And Luke chose to *sleep* down here?

The grungy, threadbare couch that I recognized from before had been dragged against the far wall, against those smooth, round, egg-like stones. It was a jaundiced shade of chartreuse, except in the places where the pilling fabric had completely worn through, spewing clouds of dirt-clotted cotton batting from frayed seams. A fringed wool blanket lay in a heap over one sunken arm, and a dented-in pillow was tossed carelessly at the other, confirming that indeed, impossibly, this was where my brother was now spending his nights.

To one side of the couch was a flimsy folding card table, and on that an ancient television set manufactured, I guessed, sometime well before the age of Technicolor. I couldn't imagine it even worked, but its nearness to the couch suggested that, indeed, my brother had been making use of it.

I inhaled, shuddering, and the heady scent of rot, of spoil, filled my lungs, oily and viscous enough to almost taste. I heard scurrying from a corner, and closed my eyes, flashing briefly to images from my recent dreams.

I didn't want to be dramatic, or *hysterical*. But in that moment, the rattling, the rustling—it sounded like rolling

(bones)

marbles?

Matchsticks?

Some other form of child's play?

It had been eons, ages, life spans past since Luke or I played with toys like those. So who was causing the rustling sound?

Fingers skated across my waist, and there was a swift, tight pinch, a twist of my skin that brought hot tears to my eyes.

I wasn't alone in Amity. Or in my own head.

Who is sharing my space?

(Whose bones were buried in this basement, Gwen?)

The sensation, those snaking fingertips, they dissipated,

266

leaving me to the echoes of my harsh breathing. My side throbbed dully in their wake. I bit back the urge to shriek.

(*Whose bones?*)

Another beat, another low, jagged breath, another flicker—

And then.

There was a gentle tap on my shoulder, a soft exhale on my cheek.

I turned to follow it, but I was still alone.

Wasn't I?

"THIS IS WHERE IT COMES FROM."

I heard the words, but there was no one beside me.

"This is where it happened. Where it always will happen."

Yes, I thought. *Of course.* Of course I'd heard the sounds, the indications of Amity's power.

The bones. The bones, and the bodies. Clattering, clanking. Creaking.

The banging of the shotgun.

The shrieking, the shouts and screams.

Angry, gnarled phantom fingers, grabbing and prying at my flesh.

The room flickered like a projection in the midst of re-adjustment. I could sense the shift in the atmosphere, the charging of particles. I could see, quite clearly, a hazy crimson curtain pass over the underground space, could make out the glimmer of a scarlet glow from beneath a crack in the wall, where stone met earthen floor.

"There."

The phantom voice was ragged. My heart rattled against my ribs. From under the wall's crack, the fault line, a slip, a scrap of paper peeked out at me. I moved toward it, tugged at it, tried to pry it free. The stone above it jiggled, showering a small dust storm down.

I leaned forward and sneezed, pulling the stone loose. Through the gaping space it left behind, I saw the corner of . . . *something*. Some kind of folder? A binder, three-ring style?

"*Yes.*" Yes, the voice was saying; *yes*, there was something there; and, *yes*, I was meant to find it. To unearth it. With only the slightest hesitation, I set about loosening the stones on either side of the fresh opening, sifting, raking at the dirt with my fingers until the object was clear to me.

It *was* a binder. Overstuffed, caked with dirt and moldy stains.

"*This is where it begins. This is where it happens. This is where it always* will *happen.*"

Always, I thought, my gorge rising.

I fished the binder out.

IT SEEMED LIKE A SCRAPBOOK, filthy white plastic, cracked at the corners and covered in mud. It reeked of decay, of the particular dead-body rot I'd come to know from my dreams.

Opening the book sent a frisson through me, an electrical charge that I felt in a tight band across my forehead. It was filled with irregular bunches of papers, some yellowed with age, some crisp, folded-over, choice phrases traced in alarm-red, accusing underline. Hole-punched newspaper articles, blurred and worn and fraying, and other clips, photo album pages with clear laminate skins curling up at the edges.

Memigassett, I read. *Burial rituals. Nexus of power.*

It was documentation, I realized, of all I'd seen in my waking dreams.

But where had it come from?

(*the red room*)

The thought was there, then gone again. But, yes, that was what lay beyond the stone barriers of Amity's basement. The red room. That was what I had seen, at night, time and time again.

"*Yes.*"

Still the voice remained disembodied, though I felt breath

against my shoulder, sensed the ruffle of air, of an arm's reach around and past me.

The scrapbook pages ruffled—on their own?

No, not on their own, Gwen, I knew. *You are not alone in Amity.*

A headline, bold and dark as a gunshot: **THE CONCORD RUNS RED AGAIN: FAMILY SLAUGHTERED AT AMITY.**

The date was ten years past. There was a picture, too. Blurry and unreliable, but chilling nonetheless.

It was a photograph of a boy just about Luke's age. It *wasn't* Luke—*that* I could see, *that* my poisoned, addled mind knew incontrovertibly—but this boy's eyes held the same dead, flat haunting look that my brother's had of late.

(*this is where it always happens*)

There was a sticky note superimposed toward the bottom of the clip. I recognized the handwriting, identified the green, rounded script as Aunt Ro's. *Curse?* she'd written. *Ten-year cycle?*

Land = danger?

Had she brought this information with her on her visit? She must have. How it had ended up in this scrapbook, hidden *inside* the red room, I couldn't say for certain.

But I thought it had to do with Luke.

"Yes."

Another breath, another sigh, another turn of the page. More pleading missives from Ro addressed to my mother but never delivered, clearly. And over that, something else, something that sent shock waves through my bones, that made my toes tighten and flex.

Heavy, dark, angry scrawls, the impression of the pen nearly bursting through the paper.

NSIZEGW. The lettering peaked into jagged points, accusing arrows.

The handwriting was Luke's. But a mad Luke, a Luke not in his right mind.

"Eyes," I heard. "It means eyes."

Eyes, yes: below the lettering, Luke had sketched a side view of Amity herself, her winking side windows peering out, searching, surveying the landscape . . . like eyes.

And beneath that: 3:14.

IT WAS THE FRANTIC SHRIEK OF THE TEAKETTLE that pulled me back to the present, startling me from the siren-lit shadows of the cellar. Without thinking, I dropped the scrapbook

(*where did it come from?*)

and rushed upstairs.

It took me a full moment, a complete breath in and out again, to realize the kitchen floor was wet.

Wet and warm, a puddle pooling out from the center of the room where Luke stood, a stream spouting from the mouth of the silenced kettle he now held in his hands. It splashed at the tops of his feet, flushing the skin a raw, protesting red.

I screamed.

Immediately, my mother appeared. "Luke!" She wrestled the kettle from him on impulse, then realized how utterly white-hot it was. She dropped it to the floor with a loud clang, shrieking herself.

"I'll get something," I said, shock giving way to action. I raced to the freezer to pull out something, anything at all.

Luke seemed numb as Mom walked him to the kitchen table, pulling out a chair for him to sit on, and another on which she propped his scalded legs. He blinked as I draped a bag of frozen peas across one, and a supermarket-sticky broccoli blend on the other, but didn't say anything.

And he didn't seem to feel any pain.

"What were you doing, Luke? What happened?" Mom asked, her voice uneven. I imagined my own history of skittish, unexplainable behavior had increased her sensitivity. But she didn't expect this sort of thing from Luke, obviously.

The only sound in the room was the intermittent pulse of the last remaining drops from the kettle, and my own confused, labored breathing. Finally, Luke tilted his head. He bent forward, retrieving the bag of broccoli from his leg and examining it with curiosity. Where the bag had been, his skin was raw, pink, and puffy.

His gaze skated over me, past me, and beyond, not taking me in—not taking *anything* in. "I really should go. Too much to do. Shovel's in the boathouse."

Mom's mouth dropped open. I frowned.

(*where did the scrapbook come from?*)

(*shovel's in the boathouse*)

(*this is where it happens, Gwen*)

He stood, letting the frozen vegetables splat wetly against the floor.

He left the room without another word.

MY MOTHER DIDN'T MEET MY EYES as she rose and replaced the vegetables in the freezer. I wondered if she, too, had been disturbed in her sleep by visions or unsolicited visits from the shadows and ciphers that clung to Amity's dank, rotted corners.

I wondered what she would say if I showed her the scrapbook I'd found.

Or the passage to the red room.

I wondered, but knew better than to ask.

Instead, I called Aunt Ro.

TEN YEARS EARLIER
DAY 17

CONNOR

BY MY THIRD WEEK IN AMITY, MY DREAMS WERE ALL REGULAR ENOUGH that they didn't feel so much like dreams anymore. They were more like some kind of streaky, heavy trip, one that lasts way too long.

They were actually sort of fun.

I learned to expect them. And from there it got so I was like maybe even *craving* them. Like whatever was happening in the dreams, whatever energy I was pulling from the house, I mean, it was building me up.

Something was happening to me in those dreams. Something powerful. Powerful, and dangerous.

Amity was showing me—she was *telling* me—because she was trying to rile me up, like. Showing me, like I say, my father's true nature.

My father's true nature, and my own.

SO IT WAS NIGHT—THE *DEAD* OF NIGHT, LIKE THEY SAY—AND JULES WAS THERE, BUT NOT THERE.

This was the not-real Jules, but she was still almost *more* real to me than life awake. I sensed her, strong like a hurricane even, before I actually saw her.

It was the goddamn banging sound that woke me again—the boathouse door slamming away.

I turned toward my nightstand. *3:14.*

Always 3:14. It was like a regular wake-up call.

Or, I guess, the call to my real-reality, I mean. It was getting harder—like even harder than usual—to tell the difference. The more time I spent at Amity, *in* Amity, the more it all ran together.

And the more it ran together, the less I minded.

I got up, moved toward the window, pressing my hand flat against the window and looked outside. From the river, this hazy mist drifted up. It made me think of smoke signals, like you'd read about in old Indian legends, you know?

Maybe someone was trying to send me a message.

The idea made me smile. And then the mist was moving, just wiggling its way along to the house. All crooked, like a beckoning finger.

It was *creeping.*

Toward *me*.

I felt the weight of Jules right behind me. "The mist," I said. "It looks like a message."

It is. Jules's voice was thick. *Are you afraid?*

"No."

Good, she said. *Then let's go.*

I have something to show you.

I BLINKED, or maybe, like, looked away, just for a second, I mean, and then we were on the other side of that stone wall.

The red room. Being inside it was like coming home.

The proportions of the room were jerky and confusing; from one angle it was low and narrow, like a crawl space, but if I just turned an inch or two, the ceiling stretched, towering over me.

I reached out with both arms, brushing my fingertips along the walls. My nails caught on little trace markings, cave drawings or something, like a kind of proof, real primitive, that this place was really here. That *I* was here, in one reality or another.

The dirt was cold and crumbly underneath my bare feet. I flexed my toes, thinking about worms, you know, and other things that lived in the ground. I knew there were bones, bodies, lurking down there. Rolling around underneath me.

Waiting for me to find them.

This is where they were buried, Con, Jules said, *Here.*

It was like a curtain parted, right in front of me, so I could see exactly what she meant, what she—and the mist, and Amity, herself, what all of them—were trying to tell me:

Torn-up death shrouds, strings of chipped shells. Iron clamps, all rusted up and crusted over. I could *smell* it: disease, death. Older than anything. Older than forever.

This is where the massacre rained down.

Jules's image floated next to me, sort of transparent. Her mouth didn't open when she spoke, but I heard her perfect inside my head just the same.

This is where they hid for safety—

—Seeking out respite.

—Seeking out revenge.

You see?

I did.

I saw my father, and I saw myself, my hands slick, sticky, and stinking that bright, coppery blood smell. I knew right away that the blood on my hands was my father's, not my own.

Jules pointed.

I saw:

The shovel. My shovel.

Dig. Jules was speaking for Amity now.

And I was acting for all of us.

Dig, she said again. *There's something buried here for you.*

I GASPED, HACKED, AND SPUTTERED, and I was in my bedroom again, suddenly. I was bolt upright in bed, the sheets a sweaty mess at my ankles, the banging of the boathouse door sounding more like gunshots than ever.

I blinked and turned to the clock.

3:14.

Of course.

With one last angry crash, the banging outside stopped. I flinched, then laughed at myself in the darkness.

You imagined it all, Connor.

You're losing it now. Just completely letting go, giving in to the voices in your head.

Digging something up in the red room? A crawl space between the walls? That's not reality. You're hallucinating. And that's what crazy people do.

Monsters.

It was what the counselors would've said. But it was still damn near impossible to convince myself.

I wasn't sure I *wanted* to convince myself.

But if I'd been inside the red room, if I'd used the shovel, then . . . where was whatever I dug up? I was alone, in my bedroom, just a normal guy in the normal, real world.

The reality and the waking dreams, they were bleeding

together so much lately. It was confusing me, making me feel all blurry. Making me feel like I needed to do something strong, something powerful, just to snap myself back into place.

I reached to pull the sheets back up over myself.

My hands touched something cold and firm. Something metal.

I froze.

It was a shotgun.

In my bed. Next to me.

It was a shotgun, caked in dirt.

A crawl space between the walls. Digging something up. Something that Amity wanted for me to have.

It was crazy thinking, okay, yeah. It didn't make sense.

But the gun was here. Cold, solid steel against my palm.

I wrapped one finger around the trigger.

And smiled.

DAY 18

IT WAS THE SOUND OF ABEL CRYING that woke me up. When I went downstairs to the kitchen, I found him in Mom's lap, whimpering. Jules was standing over them, pressing an ice cube wrapped in a paper towel to his lip.

His swollen, bloody lip.

Jeez, there was a lot of blood, drying all in a clumpy beard along his chin. It looked kind of cool, honestly.

"What happened?" I asked, trying not to stare too hard at all of the blood.

"It's nothing," Mom said quickly. "Abel slipped."

Jules rolled her eyes at me.

Slipped. Right. "Into Dad's fist?"

"It was my fault for getting in the way," Abel said, in the smallest, most little-boy voice he had. It got to me, just a little, which was kind of a surprise. "I didn't mean to run into him. I was looking for Mommy."

Mom smoothed her hand over Abel's forehead. "It's okay," she said, in her mother-hen tone. "But I don't know what you were so upset about."

She looked up at Jules. "He came streaking into the bedroom like he'd seen the devil."

Maybe he did, I thought.

From against Mom's shirt, Abel sniffed. "I hate this place. There are bad things here hiding everywhere. I hear them at night."

Mom shushed him. "Your father will be mad if he hears you saying stuff like that. There's nothing bad here. Get that idea out of your head."

He hiccupped, and Mom scooted him off her lap. "Let's go rest for a little while," she said and pulled him away. She flashed a last empty kind of look at Jules and me and then they were gone. Jules and I were alone.

"Pretty screwed up," I said, after a beat.

"Well, yeah." Jules sighed. She ran her fingers through her hair, then stretched her arms high above her head. "What the hell was he talking about, Con? I mean, really?"

"The kid's six, Jules." I stared at her, hard. "'Course he's hearing ghosts in the corners. He lives with the freaking boogeyman, right? The kid knows from evil."

He lives with the boogeyman. . . . And he lives with me.

At Amity.

Jules bit her lip. I could read my sister pretty well. Right then I had a feeling she was thinking about those squirrels, that shovel, all of the blood, and the mess. . . .

I had a feeling she was thinking about falling, getting pulled into the river that day.

She sighed again. "I just . . . well. Whatever karma is coming to bite Dad in the ass, I hope it gets here soon."

I looked at her. "Right."

But all I could think was *Screw karma. I don't need karma. Just an excuse to start things off.*

And now I had one.

Just like all those years ago. Just like that time in the attic of the old house—

That excuse, it came from Jules.

Jules was the one who started it, way back when. Now I was ready to get moving, to take over. To finish the job.

It was time.

ANOTHER NIGHT, ANOTHER WAKING DREAM.

It was the scratching at my window that woke me.

I got up right away, really eager to see what the noise was. I mean, I know they say, *Curiosity killed the cat,* but . . .

I looked at the clock: *3:14. Of course.*

The window was closed—not that it helped with the cold at all, but, whatever—so I unlatched it and slid it up so that I could look outside.

First, the sky was all clouded over. Like you couldn't even see the stars, only fog.

And then.

Through the mist, I saw a glimmer.

No—*two* glimmers. Side by side.

Two glowing, red eyes.

Interesting.

I leaned forward, toward them, but the wind shifted. When I blinked again, the eyes—whoever, *whatever* they were—they were gone. Just vanished.

The eyes were gone. But something else was there for me.

When I turned around, Jules was waiting.

HER SKIN WAS GHOST-WHITE, and almost see-through. Her hair fell in tangles down her back.

And her shoulders . . .

Her shoulders . . .

Her shoulders were blood soaked.

"What happened?" I asked. My voice wasn't totally right. There was so much blood, like a waterfall, all down her back.

There was an accident. Jules was matter-of-fact about it, doing that talking-inside-my-head thing that happened in these dead-of-night times lately.

"Who did this?" I asked.

You know. Blood bubbled in the corner of her mouth.

"But when? Where are we?" I was shaking now, could barely choke the words out. "Are you showing me the future? Is this what's going to happen to you, Jules?"

Is it, Connor? Her voice was light and silvery. *You know what we have to do, Connor. You know what you have to do. To stop him.*

"Dad?" I sputtered. "Dad did this to you?"

He's a demon.

Fury grabbed me by the throat. "Yeah." He *was* a demon, no secret there.

You know what you have to do.

I knew: the shotgun. That's what it was for.

"I can do it," I said, my breath coming fast. "I think."

It was a lie, though. I didn't think. I *knew*. I knew all too well:

When it came to my father, I *could*. Of course I could.

I didn't need karma. Just an excuse.

An excuse, and the shotgun.

And Amity.

NOW

DAY 20

GWEN

RO'S IMMINENT ARRIVAL HAD A DIFFERENT EF-FECT, a different tone, from the first time she'd come to visit. Before our house had been light and airy in anticipation, but now the mood at Amity had soured, frayed into a stale jumble as fractured and gray as my own thoughts. Luke was all but buried alive in the basement, and my mother seemed angrier at me for noticing this than concerned by its implications.

She was worried about the visit. She'd said so to my father the night before last, hissing in frustration behind their bedroom door.

Of course, sound carries in Amity.

"I don't like it," she snapped, the breaks in her words suggesting evening rituals: bedclothes being turned down, books being stacked on a nightstand, lamps switched on or off again. "Whatever Gwen's worried about, it's nothing she didn't create for herself. She's *letting* it happen. Letting her mind go. And bringing Ro here, it just validates all of the . . . imaginary fears, the delusions. It makes her worse."

Another ominous beat.

"Maybe we should just send her back now. Laurel Valley will make the space for the right price. Maybe she needs it. She can't go on like this, you know."

(go *away, crazy*)

My throat closed, my vision narrowing to a pinprick. I *couldn't* go on like this, true. But I was deathly afraid of how the end of this, of whatever *this* actually was, might reveal itself.

A muffled hum, my father protesting. A scattered handful of clarity: "Or, she could talk Gwen down. Sometimes Ro is good at that. They're both so . . . strange. Unique, I mean. They see eye to eye."

Also true.

"I'd rather they didn't." Mom's voice was sharp as razor wire. "It's not healthy."

My pulse seemed to miss a beat. From across the hallway, an ornate sconce flared and popped, the bulb sizzling out, sending a hint of ash into the air.

The door to the shared bath swung closed with a clap and a rattle, and I shivered, turning.

Slowly, warily, I made my way to my bedroom. Aunt Ro would be back again, tomorrow. What happened beyond that, we'd have to see.

RO CARRIED A BAG AS SHE MOVED FROM HER CAR up the walk to the front door, a bulky linen tote that peeked out beneath her smaller woven purse. A flare of hope blossomed in my chest when I saw that bag, even as my mother sighed, breathing her warm resentment past me, over my shoulder.

Ro paused at the front door, her features tight. When she knocked, I saw more hesitation than I would have expected, than I would have hoped for.

I ran to open the door—my mother made no move to do so herself—and gave Ro a small, anxious smile. "You're here." I stepped aside and ushered her in, pretending not to see how overwhelmingly ill at ease she looked.

Pretending not to feel the same way myself.

"IT'S JUST RIDICULOUS."

My mother took Ro's bags from her and set them on the tall, marble-topped console table beside the front door. "You were here, what, three weeks ago? And you were *supposed* to stay over then, too. And you blew out so suddenly, no explanation. Then you and Gwen are off having secret conversations—and you can both thank me, by the way, that the phone's back up and running. And now you come rushing out here, so dramatically. I just . . . I don't know what to make of it."

The set of her mouth said otherwise. She knew. She had formed her own opinion, and carved it out in stone. She simply wasn't happy about what she thought she knew.

"I just wanted to see her, Mom." Surely that explanation was innocent enough.

Mom ignored me, concentrating all of her energy on her sister. "We thought the move would be a fresh start. . . . We thought it would be good for Gwen." She put her hands on her hips. "I just don't understand."

Ro flashed a glance over Mom's shoulder at me.

To my mother, she said, "I know you don't."

AUNT RO ALLOWED HERSELF A GLASS OF WATER (and, I thought, a moment to gain her bearings). We sat, tense and awkward, around the kitchen table.

"Hal went to pick up some food for an early dinner," Mom said, her voice faltering slightly. "We thought barbecue. The oven's been acting up a bit."

We'd discovered the pilot light was unreliable, leaving us in constant danger of unwittingly filling the house with gas. Just another of Amity's quirks.

Ro was quiet, noncommittal. I was reaching to pour myself more water when Murray's sudden, insistent barking turned all of our attention outside, down toward the river.

Toward the boathouse.

Mom sighed. "That dog didn't take to the move very well."

"He's high-strung," I said, defensively. I could relate.

"Why don't we go check on him?" Aunt Ro tilted her head at me. "I never did see the river the last time I was here."

I swallowed.

"Okay. I'll take you."

THERE WAS A STILLNESS TO THE AIR OUTSIDE despite the way that Murray's whining grated.

I made my way down the grassy slope barefoot, feeling dew squelch between my toes. Closer to the river, the grass was soggy and overgrown. Our feet sunk deeper and deeper with each step as we moved toward the shoreline.

Abruptly, Murray's whining stopped. He caught sight of me at the same time I did him, cocking his head in my direction and pawing insistently at the ground.

"What is it, boy?" I wiped the sheen of sweat from my upper lip. "What are you so upset ab—"

I saw.

IT WAS A BIRD, a heron, I thought, although I was no expert. Several feet long with a slim, pointed beak. Slender, willowy tree-branch legs. It must have been quite majestic once.

Before it was killed.

It *had* been killed, sometime recently from the looks of it. It lay on one side, talons jutting stiffly out, split open at the breastbone. Gore streaked its underside like a grotesque bib, twig-like bones peeking through the slippery mess. Its eyes were empty, bloody sockets, gazing blankly, screaming a silent accusation at me.

Murray pawed at it, sending it into a logroll downhill, trailing bright strings of viscera in its wake.

I raced to the river and vomited.

"WHAT ARE YOU DOING DOWN HERE?"

I was hunched by the edge of the river, Ro crouched beside me with a hand on my back, when we heard Luke's voice from above. I wiped a line of spit from my chin, splashed some river water on my face, and straightened to find him staring at us.

I fought the urge to flinch. Had *Luke* killed the bird? Killed it . . . and torn it apart?

My stomach gurgled again. Looking into his face and finding nothing there but pure, sharp anger, I thought it seemed possible. Probable, even, though to what end I couldn't say.

Best not to ask.

Luke shifted, regarding Ro. "Forgot you were coming." He scowled at her.

"Oh?" She didn't move to greet him. The heady, rotten-fruit smell of the bird lingered in the air.

"Murray was outside." I pushed my hair out of my eyes self-consciously. "We came to get him. Ro hadn't seen the river yet."

Luke smirked. "Well, here it is." He swept his arm toward the Concord, and the puddle of pale froth that was my vomit. Shame licked at my cheeks.

"And here *he* is." He pointed to Murray, who now cow-

299

ered at Ro's side, giving my brother a wide berth. "Take him away, would you? He's in the way."

In the way of what? I didn't ask, just nodded and slapped at my thigh. "Come on, Murray."

The dog gave me a baleful look, slinking to me in slow motion. His ears remained flattened against his head, and his teeth were ever-so-slightly bared.

Luke didn't appear to notice.

"Your mother says you've been digging up the boathouse floor," Ro said. Her voice was broken glass, a rusty chain turning slowly on an ancient, twisted gear.

"It was all rotted out," Luke said. He wouldn't meet her eyes. "I'm rebuilding. People who lived here before, they kept a junker boat out here. We could fix it up, you never know." His lips moved independent of the rest of his face, telling a different story from the rest of his body.

"You never know," Ro agreed. "Found anything interesting in there?"

Interesting. The word filled my head with crashing waves.

Luke squinted. "Oh, sure. Lots of stuff."

"Such as?"

Luke shrugged, those churning waves coming over me again, tossing me against the invisible pilings of an imaginary pier. He glanced at the boathouse, then turned back to me, heat rushing between us like a missile.

"Old things."

LUKE WAS FINISHED TALKING TO US, so he turned and wandered away. Ro, Murray, and I made our way back up the hill, toward the house, with near-perfect synchronicity.

Ro paused and reached for my hand, giving it a squeeze.

"Gwen," she said, her tone strained. "Maybe you should stay away from the boathouse. Stay away from Luke when he's down there, I mean."

My stomach clenched. *Or else what?* I thought wildly. *What?*

He keeps things in there, a voice whispered, light as the breeze against my cheek. *He finds things. Deadly things.*

I whipped my head around, but saw nothing.

"Are you all right?" Ro asked, her eyes tracking the direction the voice had come from.

"I thought . . ." I pulled away, withdrew my hand from her grip. "It's fine," I said. "It's nothing. I'll stay away from the boathouse. I promise."

I didn't ask why. I had an idea that I'd find out what Ro meant soon enough.

RO SAID SHE WAS GOING TO TAKE A NAP before dinner, and when she stretched her slender arms up, I felt exhaustion clutch me, skating the length of my body. I said I thought that sounded like a good idea, ignoring the inverted V that my words knit into Mom's forehead.

The doctors had explained that excessive sleep and sluggishness were telltale signs of depression.

But there was certainly no harm in an innocent afternoon rest.

I wasn't the one digging through the boathouse floor, after all. Yet Luke's behavior was above reproach. Luke wasn't the crazy one.

Only the one to be avoided, evidently.

"I left your bags in Luke's bedroom," Mom said to Ro, nodding in the general direction of the staircase. "The sheets are clean."

"Luke's bedroom? Oh no. I don't want to put him out," Ro protested.

"You won't," I said. "He sleeps in the basement now."

"Ah." She pursed her lips. "Siesta, then, shall we? Come get me when you wake up, Gwen, so we can gossip."

"I don't have anything to gossip about. No stories." Nothing light or easy anyway.

"I doubt that."

"Really," I insisted.

It *wasn't* exactly the truth, but it was what my mother wanted to hear. Her worry lines relaxed a fraction.

Aunt Ro gave a halfhearted smile. "Okay, then," she said. "You can do the listening."

I'D THOUGHT I WAS BONE-TIRED, but once I was in bed, sleep was reluctant to come. The sunlit patterns on the walls seemed wrong. Uneasy, as though Amity were only meant to exist in the dark. Though my windows were open, the blinds were drawn, and a steady breeze flapped them against the window frames in rhythmic time, a watered-down, daylight version of the boathouse door.

When I closed my eyes, the heron appeared, gaping, bloodied eye sockets yawning open, threatening to swallow me, to surround the whole house and devour us, eat us alive.

When I closed my eyes, the girl from the mirror—from the woods, from my nightmares—revealed herself, purplish clots of blood trickling down her shoulders, shiny and freshly let.

Old things, she hissed as a beetle waved a spindly tentacle from the corner of one unfocused eye.

Behind my eyelids, the Concord River rushed red.

Then, through the haze, I heard my name, sharp and shrill.

MY FIRST THOUGHT was that I'd imagined the sound of my name, that plaintive, earnest call. The air felt still as an underground grotto, still as the cellar of Amity could be.

Then it came again, louder, more urgent: *"Gwen!"*—and beyond it, my mother's rapid-fire footsteps slammed against the stairs.

Luke's room. It was where the voice had come from, where my mother was headed now. It was where Aunt Ro was staying.

I flew from my bed, through the bathroom, and toward my aunt.

"STOP SCREAMING!"

My mother's voice rang out with anger. "What on *earth*, Ro?" She grabbed her sister by the shoulders and shook hard. Ro pushed at Mom's arms wildly, pulling free, sitting up straight in bed.

"Are you *insane?*" Mom demanded, flinching when she realized her word choice. It sliced at me, making my shoulders hunch.

"You have to calm down. You *know* Gwen's prone to . . ." She paused, groping for the word that was always, *always*, on the tip of my tongue, on the edge of my brain, dancing at the periphery of my existence. ". . . *hysteria.*"

Hysteria. The sounds, the syllables, they rushed inside my head. The rotted-fruit smell from outside, from before, filled my nostrils, making me want to swoon.

"What happened, Ro? What did you need?" Mom sat at the end of the bed, smoothing out the covers around her.

"I *needed* to talk to Gwen," Ro said. "I apologize for yelling." She bit her lip. "No, never mind. I take that back, Ell. *Of course* I yelled."

She took a deep breath. "It's this house," she said. "Don't you feel it?"

Dimly, the static-charge sensation began to gather inside me.

"You *do*. I know you do." Ro was talking to me.

She sighed. "Ellen, this house is . . . *poisoned*. I don't think it's good for Luke. And it's tearing Gwen apart."

I closed my eyes. *The heron. The mirror-girl. The bloody river. The shotgun.*

"What do you see, Gwen?" Ro asked softly, making me start.

"Ro, that's enough—"

The static crackled, tunneling through me and exploding, firing underneath my skin.

"It's *not* enough, Ellen, not remotely. There's something wrong with this place. It's been there since day one, and you can't ignore it! Why do you think she called me? You have to stop pretending. You *have* to. Even if you're scared, even if you don't understand. Be honest: Gwen is different, and this place . . . it's dangerous."

"Dangerous to Gwen." My mother sniffed, her face stony.

"Dangerous to *all* of you," Ro corrected. "How much do you know about this house? The realtor must've given you some of the history, right? She must have told you why it was so underpriced?" She flushed. "I wanted to say something. I was going to tell you last time. I brought papers, things I'd found."

The scrapbook. Ro's handwriting. Pages stashed away in Luke's secret cache. She had wanted to warn us.

Now her skin blazed fiery. "The papers I brought . . . disappeared. And then, well . . . I had to leave."

Not disappeared, I thought. *They were hidden. By Luke. By Amity.*

She wanted me to know the truth only on her own terms. And Amity got what she wanted.

Mom faltered. "The realtor mentioned . . . structural issues. She said there might be some costs later on." Mom was lying, I thought. Or at least holding something back.

Ro snorted. "Structural issues. Try an entire underground dugout. It housed accused refugees during the Salem witch trials. And later, this place was an asylum. One of the doctors on staff went crazy, began doing medical experiments, torturing some of the clinically insane patients in secret down there."

The bones. The whispers. The messages, the scrawls on the mirror, the echoes of a long-ago shotgun. The forces, building around me.

Building inside me, boiling to a fever pitch.

"All houses have histories," my mother said, her voice lower now, shaky. "It wasn't a reason not to buy. The witch trials were hundreds of years ago! This house didn't even exist then."

"*It's not about the house,* Ellen. It's more than that. This site, it's rotted. People think it's cursed. People think it's *evil.*"

That seemed to snap my mother back to the concrete, to reason and rationale. "I can't, Ro." She waved a hand and gathered a hank of hair from her face, raising her chin defiantly, eyes flashing. "You have to stop. That's ridiculous."

"It's not." Ro stood. "I wish it were. Are you deliberately avoiding the truth? Do you know how many people have died in this place? It wasn't just the witches, or the mental patients. *Do you know what happened to the last family who lived here?*"

The buzz gathered, pressing against my skull like a vise. Above us, Luke's light fixture flickered, rattling like a pot lid under steam pressure.

"I'll show you." Hands on her hips, Ro's eyes darted across the room. "I brought more books about it. The Concord Library lost their records in a flood—what a surprise—but the information's still out there. When Gwen called, I dug it up again. Where did you put my bags?"

Confused, my mother glanced at the bed. "I left everything there. On the floor by the nightstand."

The space was empty now. Fear licked at me, scratched at my ankles, trailing jagged claw marks along the tops of my bare feet.

"You must have moved them," my mother said.

"Of course I didn't," Ro replied. "Why would I?" She folded her arms. "I was going to show you. Well, first, I was going to show Gwen. I knew she'd believe me. Though I have a feeling she knows enough about things as it is."

The room shrunk in, grew dimmer, and Ro's voice unraveled at half tempo. *I* unraveled, a fiber-optic spiderweb draping me in a shimmering net. Overhead, the light blacked out, then switched back on more weakly, soaking us in an eerie, alien glow.

"Maybe Luke moved them. Maybe he put them in the closet," my mother offered.

Ro shot her a look. "When was the last time Luke came up here?"

My mother said nothing. Her skin was sallow but for two bright splotches of pink high in her cheeks.

"Fine," Ro conceded, doubtful. "I'm telling you, I didn't

move them. But if it will satisfy you, I'll check the closet right now."

The room washed red. Pain twitched, then exploded at the base of my skull.

(she was shot in the HEAD THE HEAD THE HEAD)

Don't go in there—I tried to form words but they clung to my tongue.

Ro stepped into the closet.

Invisible hands, cold and lifeless, closed around my throat. I couldn't scream, couldn't breathe. The overhead light sizzled and cracked, bulbs blacking.

Don't don't DON'T—

The door slammed shut behind her.

THE DOORKNOB RATTLED, shaking the heavy, solid wood, but the closet door held firm. Then came a distinct *thud*, the solid, meaty sound of flesh being slapped, slammed up against unyielding substance that could only be Ro throwing herself against it. The door held fast.

"They're not here!" she cried. "The closet is empty! Open the door!"

"We didn't close it!" My mother sounded unsure now. "It's not locked!"

The sour, metallic bite of copper flooded my mouth, thick and runny like I was choking on blood.

(*the head the head the head*)

"It won't open," Ro said, fingernails scrabbling against the doorknob. *"Unlock the door!"*

The space beneath the closet door glowed scarlet, feral, and urgent, and a growl rose up—not quite human, not quite not—from beneath the floorboards, from deep within the bowels of the house. Inside the closet, Ro sobbed freely, babbling in incoherent mumbles that rose, gathering intensity by the second.

"Rosemary!" My mother's voice had taken on a clipped bark that belied her own rare fright. She grabbed at the doorknob and gasped, pulling back, like she'd plunged her hand directly into a furnace, or tried to clasp an open flame between her fingers.

"Try to relax, Ro," my mother pleaded.

The buzzing, louder now, chattered and rose, beckoning from outside of me, from the direction of the closet.

I watched, transfixed, as a swarm of hornets poured from underneath the door.

I screamed.

The door flew open, revealing my aunt, staggering forward as though prodded by invisible hands.

Ro's face was studded with stings.

She was so swollen with bumps and bruises that she was nearly unrecognizable, a melted wax image, the skin on one eyelid stretched red and puffy, tight as a straitjacket. Her good eye, impossibly round, stared out from the bloated, mottled bread loaf that her face had become.

"There's nothing in there," she croaked, opening her mouth wide. A torrent of blood gushed out.

My entire body clenched. Involuntarily, my limbs jerked straight and stiff, my head snapped back, and my teeth gnashed together hard enough to chip several.

The ceiling light twisted and rotated on its base.

With an explosive, violent roar, it came crashing to the ground.

THE LAMP MISSED US BY INCHES.

That was what my mother told me when I came to again.

I'D ONLY BEEN OUT FOR A FEW MINUTES, she said—
not even enough time for her really to worry, given how dis-
traught Ro was when she finally emerged from the closet.

Mom had fully regained her composure now, one hand
resting against the sharp angle of her hip bone, the other
nursing the cup of water Ro brought up to the bedroom with
her when she first came upstairs.

I blinked at my mother's blasé reaction to Ro's stings. She
no longer looked like a carnival sideshow freak, true—maybe
some of the wasp bites died down after the initial sting—but
there was still that one eye, fat and red as a tomato, slit shut
clamshell tight. Ro pressed her index and middle fingers gingerly to the wound, offering me a wary look with her good,
open eye.

"I . . . fainted?" I glanced around the room. "You were in
the closet," I said to Aunt Ro. "You were stuck."

"I was stuck," she confirmed through cracked, blistered
lips. "Locked in."

My mother frowned. "No one locked you in. The doors
don't even have locks here. It's an old house, Ro. The wood
warps. You just insist on overreacting. I wish I could say it was
unlike you."

Ro's expression was sour. "You'd never say that, Ells. Just

admit it. You think overreacting is *exactly* like me. Remember? It's why you didn't want me coming, riling poor, fragile Gwen up."

My mother's features hardened. "Fine. If you want to be blunt, then. Yes. It's ridiculous, you streaking out here like a lunatic, books and papers and whatever other horrible stories about this house.

"It doesn't *matter* what happened here before, Ro. Houses don't have energy, or memory, or whatever it is you're worried about. There's *nothing to be afraid of* here. *Amity is only a house.*" Her face shone sweaty and tight with emotion.

"But . . . Ro's face," I stammered. "The wasps." Regardless of where they came from, either the natural world or the depths of Amity herself . . . Surely my mother could see that the wasps were dangerous. That was just a fact.

Ro flashed me a knowing look through her ruined, funhouse features.

My mother sighed, end-of-her-rope weary. She looked at me with free, unfettered anger.

She said, "*What* are you talking about, Gwen?"

"HER FACE," I REPEATED, my voice small. "Her *eye*."

I stepped forward, toward the bed, and reached out to Ro's face, tracing a tentative path across the swollen flesh, puffed and rising from the socket like a helium balloon. "We have to do something about the stings."

My mother grabbed at my elbow. "*Gwen*. That's *enough*." To Ro, she snapped, "You see?"

She meant, *You see how fragile she is? How easy it would be to break her?*

You see how she is, in fact, already broken?

Panic bubbled in my throat. The wasps, the cloud, the hum . . . the *bites*, scarring Ro's face.

My mother couldn't see them. My mother couldn't see what Amity had done.

"*No,*" I gasped, and raised a hand to my mouth as my gorge rose yet again.

"GWEN ISN'T THE PROBLEM HERE," Ro said, resigned. She flicked her eyes toward the lamp, smashed to crystal smithereens in the middle of the bedroom floor. "Actually, she might be the only one with the power to resist the house in any real way."

My mother's face paled, and her lips parted. "Stop. Talking. *Crazy*," she whispered, cold. "Just stop. I don't want to hear any more." She swallowed, eyes flashing. "Get up. And *get out*."

Ro's eyes widened. "Look, I'm sorry. I am. But I can't—I shouldn't. Not now. Gwen—"

"*Gwen* is already about fifteen times worse off than she was before you came back here," Mom said. "She doesn't need your magical voodoo talk! The lamp *fell*, the door *stuck*, and there is *nothing wrong with the house*. The only thing wrong is with Gwen's mind, which you know well enough, and having you here is obviously more dangerous for her than anything else." She pushed me aside, grabbing Ro and dragging her to her feet. "So just find your bags—or *don't*, I don't care, if it's only going to lead to another scene—and go."

I WATCHED FROM THE WINDOW OF THE SEWING ROOM as Ro's car sputtered back down our driveway. We didn't have a chance to say any kind of private good-bye.

I DREAMED OF LUKE THAT NIGHT.

The hands on my bedside clock turn over, pointing, accusing, to 3:14. Luke stands over me, cheekbones streaked with war paint, eyes glowing, body bathed in moonlight. He holds a mirror to my face.

In the dream, my reflection plays back to me: red-rimmed eyes, slit pupils, lips curled in a menacing snarl.

In the dream, I see myself as Luke sees me:

(insane)

(crazy)

Monstrous.

In the dream, I am monstrous.

But Luke?

Luke is a demon.

And he means to destroy me.

From the corner of the bedroom, Aunt Ro whispers.

Remember, *she says,* what it is that you can do.

Remember.

Soon.

Or run.

In the dream she disappears, dissolves into thin air. I am left alone, wrapped only in a bedsheet, as in her wake, Luke looms.

He raises the shotgun to eye level.

He is tall,
taller,
tallest.
He says:
"Sorry, sis."

TEN YEARS EARLIER
DAY 24

CONNOR

JULES COMES TO ME every night. At 3:14, she's there.

She says: *It's time.*

The shotgun rests, cold and still against my leg.

I tap at it, eager.

Yeah, I think. *It's time.*

PART IV

CONCORDANCE

DAY 28
(ALWAYS)

12:08

Jules sees the light on in my bedroom, peeks her head in. "Sleeping up here tonight?"

Her tone reminds me that this is unusual these days. My behavior's been unusual, I mean.

More unusual these days.

I smile at her. "Lots to do tonight." Under the covers, I wrap a hand around the butt of the shotgun.

She screws her face up. She looks puzzled, like she doesn't remember about our plans, all the stuff we talked about. But that doesn't bother me.

12:43

After tossing and turning for over an hour, I pad downstairs, ignoring the creeping sensation of being watched that permeates the air. I pour myself a glass of lukewarm water from the kitchen tap, avoiding reflective surfaces for fear of what they may reveal.

As I move back toward the hallway, the cellar door opens, and Luke bursts through.

His hair is askew, his eyes are bloodshot.

He looks at me, but doesn't seem to register. He pushes past me, determined.

I ask, "Where are you going?"

I wonder, *Now?*

He doesn't reply as he storms toward the door, down to the boathouse.

1:23

No chance of sleep. Not with Dad's snoring echoing down the hall, his breathing thick and muddy.

Not with knowing this'll be the last night that I ever hear that sound.

2:36

I realize tonight is the first night I can't hear the banging of the boathouse door, despite Luke's silhouette casting long, mutant shadows through the knots in the weathered wood.

It isn't a comforting thought.

2:42

Mom, Abel, and Dad are sleeping the sleep of the dead, thanks to some pills mixed into the water pitcher at dinner.

Mom really should keep her meds locked up.

With her and Abel out of the way, there's no reason that this—that *tonight*—shouldn't work.

2:58

Luke is planning something out in the boathouse. Plotting. With Amity.

Luke is not in his right mind tonight. And I may never have been, may never have had a right mind.

He keeps things in the boathouse. That was what Ro thought. And the ax has been missing from the woodpile for quite some time now.

3:04

Lightning bursts across the sky, and thunder claps like a gun-shot. All month now the storm's been waiting, gathering strength. Building up to this moment.

Out the window, those wild, red eyes are back. They narrow at me.

I nod back. *I understand. Yeah. Now.*

3:06

The sky is marbled with clouds and the air feels heavy, thick.
Charged.
    I think that it is going to rain.
    No.
    I think that it is going to storm.

3:11

Jules taps me on the shoulder. She's just an outline, like, buzzing in and out. I reach out to touch her and kick something cold and stiff.

The shotgun, barrels oiled and gleaming.

3:12

There is a tap on my shoulder. A breath against my ear.

A whisper:

"You have to leave, Gwen.

"You have to find a way to stop this.

"Or else—

"You have to leave."

The voice is Annie's. But when I turn to face her, to ask her to explain, the kitchen is empty.

No Annie. No Ro. No parents.

Luke is still outside.

And the rain still falls.

3:13

I don't remember leaving my room.

But suddenly, I'm in the upstairs hallway, floorboards popping under my feet. The sound, the twisting and wrenching . . . the snarls and growls of the house . . . they're not human.

Amity's *in*human. More than human. And she's inside of me.

I'm inhuman right now, too.

I make my way down the hall in the direction of our parents' bedroom, slowly, soothed by the sound of heavy, hard rain.

At their door, I wait for a minute.

My finger twitches on the trigger. Then I feel breathing on the back of my neck.

I turn and there's Jules. The *real* Jules. She's wide-eyed, scared-looking.

"What's going on, Connor?" she asks, her voice choked. "What are you doing?"

She looks down, sees the gun, and her chest starts to rise, all fast and frantic. *"What the hell is that?"*

Her voice is shrill. My face turns inside out, like my thoughts.

I say, "What do you mean?"

I press my palm into the butt of the gun, firm. "I'm doing what you told me to do. What you *asked* me to do. What we *talked* about."

She shakes her head, face white.

"Connor," she gasps. "We never talked about this. I would *never* ask you for this."

She looks dizzy. And suddenly I feel drugged, confused. Woozy.

I step closer to her. I raise the gun.

"We *planned* this," I insist. "It was your idea."

Jules grabs.

"Connor," she says, "this would *never* be my idea."

She swallows. Her fear is the sound of sandpaper, or dust.

"Connor," she says, "what are you thinking?"

But my sister, my twin . . . she *knows*.

What I'm thinking is exactly what she's always feared.

3:14

I hear a clicking sound, a particularly loud crash of thunder. A jagged streak of lightning forks across the sky.

She was shot in the head, I know, at precisely this moment. Now.

She was shot in the head.

The boathouse door bangs open, then closed again, mute against the raging of the storm.

Luke is out there, Annie says. *With the ax.*

She was shot in the head, I agree.

And we're next.

3:14

Jules lunges for the shotgun but I pull back, on instinct. Outside, the storm explodes.

I close my eyes and feel thunder blast straight through my body.

When I open them again, Jules is gone.

No, not *gone*.

Dead.

Jules is dead, her eyes empty, rolled back in her head, her mouth pinched up. Blood runs down her shoulders, pooling around her on the floor.

I'm covered in Amity, wearing her like a second skin, feeling her movements when I breathe.

Knowing: Amity is at peace.

3:21

It is Annie who tells me it is time to get out.

She's back again, flickering translucent in the dim light of the kitchen.

"*Run,*" she says, her voice a hoarse whisper. "*Now.*"

She seems to have an idea that this will be my only chance. That this moment is the end.

"*I can't,*" I say.

Overhead, the light buzzes a dull, dying fluorescent hue, coating the room in a pale, jaundiced shade. In that buttery static, Annie mutates like a shadow puppet, shifting and humming in and out of frequency. In this instant, it is easy to believe that she isn't real. That none of this is.

Then she extends an arm.

"*Gwen,*" she says, and now her voice is the sound of chains dragged against asphalt—"*you* have *to go.*"

Her fingers are greasy and cold against my palm, and as our skin makes contact, a blinding flash triggers in my mind. A bloody tableau is revealed.

(*She was shot in the head.*)

A limp, lifeless figure, glassy eyes rolled back to the whites, blood lacing the tangles of her shoulder-length curls.

A trail of gore leaking back, peaking toward a far bedroom on Amity's second floor.

The walls of the kitchen curl inward, and the cellar door creaks open.

There is a *pop*, a burst, as the room dives into inky darkness, and then back to the hazy, newspaper-yellowed tint of moments ago. I bite back the urge to shriek, to peel my own skin from my bones.

What if?

What if this were only a bad dream? What if Annie, if *Amity*—what if none of that were real?

What if Luke weren't, just now, down in the boathouse, digging? Considering things like axes, shotguns, silencers, the speed at which sound should carry across the surface of the water?

What if there were no red room? No sacred history, or stale, stained soil?

What if I really *were* crazy?

What if, what if, what—

if?

I hear a scream.

I race outside.

The storm is here.

3:40

I tear downhill, toward the boathouse, feet slipping, kicking up thick clumps of mud. I stumble, and slide down the last few paces angled on one hip, stray stones and twigs poking at me, scraping and rending my flesh as I skid along.

I slam to a halt just before the boathouse, palms raw and ankles, knees, and shins torn bloody. Wincing, I press up just enough on my forearms and rise. Push wet straggles of hair out of my eyes, blink through the torrents of rainfall.

Focus.

Before me, on the ground. Drowned in overflow from the rainfall, but dead long earlier. Head rotated fully, twisted unnaturally so that his gaze falls directly over his shoulder, directly behind him. Ax protruding from his belly, staining it sunset-whorls of reddish pink.

Murray.

I choke back a sob. *Murray.*

Luke.

I pull the door to the boathouse open and step inside.

3:45

Stop screaming! I think, my mother's words to Ro.

But I'm the one who's screaming now. And I can't seem to stop.

The boathouse floor is gone; every last rotted baseboard has been pried up, the ground turned over, raked, and razed.

Before me lies a cluster of bones.

The skeletal figure is barely larger than my own frame, and though her flesh has decayed, her clothing hangs in blood-streaked tatters. Thinning wisps of auburn curls splay out, curtains flanking a shattered skull, a fiery ring around a bull's-eye gunshot wound.

Beside her, the ragged, stained stuffed animal lies, the one I found on the road, in the woods. I reach to pick it up, fingering the pilled, worn fabric, drawing back from the fresh bloodstains that transfer to my fingertips.

I squint, rub my eyes.

Beneath the animal, there is a book.

Luke's book. *Amity's* book. The scrapbook of her history.

I pick it up, peel open the front cover, warped, more discolored than I remember. I flip, flip, flip, to the back of the book, to that one article.

FAMILY SLAUGHTERED AT AMITY.

Names. I scan them quickly, frantic.

Julianne Webb.

"Annie?"

I glance up, and she is there, particles of light shimmering through the drops of rain that sluice down her shoulders.

Jules, now. She shrugs. *Jules, always. To him.*

I think, *She was shot in the head.*

Annie—Jules—points to her figure, a heap of bones beneath the surface of Amity, another blood sacrifice.

It was an accident, she says. *He buried me.*

And then he killed the rest of them.

Annie meets my eyes, sure and strong in the moment. *I tried to help you. Jules . . .* she's angry. *The way she—we—died, she can't help anyone. But I tried.*

She glances toward the door as it swings open one last time. It trembles, shudders on its hinges, then rips savagely off its frame, and is carried away. Through the mouth of the crumbling doorway, we can just make out Luke's figure, staggering up the slope of the hill, ax in hand.

Staggering toward Amity.

Annie says one last thing:

It's happening again.

This is where it always ends, Gwen.

And with another clap of thunder, she's gone.

3:49

Thunder blasts the horizon. Swollen purple bruises cloud the sky, rolling, gathering force. Hard rain drives down, and lightning slices relentlessly at the air. I race toward Amity, toward Luke and his ax. Through sheets of rain, he screams at me, howls, contorts.

He swings the ax and misses, the blade whistling past my ear, so close I can almost feel the parting of the breeze. I lunge, lose my footing. We roll back, down the sloping hill again, toward the water's edge.

Luke plunges, is submerged. And as I peer through the frothing sheen of the Concord River, the face I see beneath is not my brother's. Mud slicks his features and his eyes glow, otherworldly, laced with red.

The face I see beneath is not human at all.

I remember:

The stones. I made the stones fall.

It wasn't something I tried to remember, but I couldn't forget it, either.

Maybe the memory would save my life.

My brother's face is not human at all. He's more than human.

But remembering the stones, I think:
So am I.

3:51

A current gathers from within, warming me, winding its way to my throat.

Luke emerges from the water, sputtering.

Ax in hand, he charges for the house, barreling past me and up the hill.

He is fast, almost there. But in my own way now, I am faster.

Those charged particles, that white noise, it fills me, churns the marrow in my bones.

This is where it always ends, too.

I open my mouth to scream.

Instead, I erupt.

My rage bubbles like a volcano, primitive and filled with fury. A streak of lightning, white-hot and nuclear, splits the house in two. I shriek, flames lapping at my insides, consuming my spine as the house—as *Amity*—is devoured.

The storm funnels out, away from the house, making space for this blazing inferno I have summoned. In the smoke, symbols, signals are revealed: the thrashing tail of a prehistoric creature, the slit pupils of a demon. A skittering, skeletal human frame.

A whistling sounds and Amity's eyes—those winking, half-moon sewing room windows—they blast and shatter, fragments of glass raining sharp and deadly in a frenzied arc. Some shards graze my shoulders, my cheeks, but I don't bother to shield myself from the blows.

I want to see this. I *need* to see this.

A small, invisible hand circles my wrist. *Annie*. She is silent but with me still.

Together, we watch Amity burn.

PART V

AFTER

NOW

Dear Jules:

They brought a new girl in today. Someone we both know.

Gwendolyn Hall. The one whose family was living in Amity, the one I mentioned in my last letter.

She's like us, I think.

Or. Well. Kind of like me. Even though there aren't that many people really like me, you know?

But anyway. I told you how they only lasted twenty-eight days, right? Just like us.

Just like everyone Amity gets her claws into.

After ten years in this place—on my best behavior, mostly—the guards are pretty good to me. I get to hear some stories, sometimes. They told me about Gwen right away, right when she first got here, this morning. "Criminally insane," like me—obviously, or she wouldn't be here to begin with. Everyone got a kick out of the fact that she had a history with Amity. Like me. They thought it was pretty weird, one of those coincidences.

Just a wild coincidence, all the freaky things that happen around Amity.

I don't bother with the truth: that there's no such thing as coincidence when it comes to Amity. The truth wouldn't get me out of here any sooner. Assuming I'm ever going to get out of here at all, which, you know, I probably won't.

Who would even believe the truth anyway?

She burned the house down, can you believe it? If you told me that was even possible, that Amity was like . . . vulnerable, I guess, that way, I would've laughed. But she burned the house down. The parents and brother managed to escape, rowed to the nearest neighbors in Dad's leaky old Leeward. Their car wouldn't start so the boat was the only choice. So there's one thing Dad did right, once in his whole miserable life.

The house is gone.

But that doesn't mean Amity is . . . over.

I don't think that happens. I don't think Amity could ever really be gone.

She was hospitalized once before. Gwen, I mean. When she was younger. Believed she had, I don't know, like magic powers, like she could move objects with her mind. There's some story going around, a rain of stones over her childhood house, just out of the clear blue sky.

Crazy talk, right? So, into the loony bin she went.

They didn't cure her. Couldn't. There's no cure for that kind of damage.

I should know, right?

It's kind of like the way I was born bad. Rotten. Evil, even before . . . even before Amity came along.

Gwen and I are alike that way, you know? Who even knows where either of us'd be, if we'd never found Amity. If Amity'd never found us.

So Gwen burned Amity down. Which is weird enough, you know? But even weirder still—it happened during a thunderstorm. Flooding, up and down the Concord River: trees down, property damaged . . . and still, in the middle of it all? Amity went up in smoke.

She says she did it with her mind. Really.

Says it was the only way to save herself, to save her family from her older brother, Luke.

He was a demon, she told the doctors. Possessed. By Amity.

She found drawings, little notes and things, those articles in that scrapbook, same as I saw. In the red room, same as me. In her dreams.

The doctors think that's funny, as much as anything like that could be. The guards heard them talking.

See, the red room never showed up on any blueprints after all. Not in any city planner's records, not anywhere. And you know there's no library in Concord anymore.

So the red room never really existed to anyone other than you or me.

Or Gwen.

Or Luke.

Yeah, the guards think it's a crazy coincidence. Or maybe that's just what they say—no one wants to drag up urban legends, like it would be some kind of jinx to admit what they think about Amity.

But you and I know the truth. And I think Gwen does, too.

Actually, there's only one part of the whole story that's ha-ha funny to me, Jules. And maybe to you, too. Because you used to get me. Most of the time.

Anyway:

Gwen says she was saved, she was taught things, shown things, by a friend. A young girl named Annie.

That scrapbook, the one she says she first saw in the red room—Gwen brought it with her to the hospital. The doctors asked how she got it out of the "red room," real condescending, you know, but she didn't say. Was all clutching it to her chest, like, during intake, didn't want to let anyone else put a hand on it. It was filled with clippings, articles, photos, crap like that.

It was my scrapbook, Jules. The one I saw. When I was in the red room.

That picture of me, it's still blurry. And that article lists the whole family, all of our names. Like yours:

Julianne Webb.

But you knew that, Jules. Right?

Or maybe I should call you Annie? Who you were when you were little. Young and innocent. Before the accident. Before Amity. Gwen says you were Annie to her, and that makes sense.

I'm not sure where you are, who you are now. But I believe you can still hear me, sense me.

I believe you understood me, and that you still do.

I believe that you still exist.

But, Jules?

I believe that Amity still exists, too.

I believe that Amity is forever.

—Connor

354

EPILOGUE

HERE

Here was a house; bones of beam and joints of hardware,
stone foundation smooth, solid as the core of the earth, nestled,
pressed, cold and flat and dank against the hard-packed soil
and all of its squirming secrets.

Here was a house; sturdy on its cornerstones, shutters spread
wide, windowpanes winking against the speckled prisms of
daylight. Weather-beaten slats of knotted siding, drinking in
nightfall. Tarred shingles surveying star maps, legends shared
in the pattern of dotted constellations above.

Here was a house; not sane, not sentient, but potent,
poisonous, drenched with decay.

Here was a house of ruin and rage, of death and deliverance,
seated atop countless nameless unspoken souls.

Here was a house of vengeance and power, land laid claim
by wraiths and ciphers, persistent and insistent, branded and

bonded and bound.

Here are remains.
Here remains.
Here is more than physical matter.
More than layers of surface
or structure
or cell.

Here is where I live, not living.

Here is always mine.

ACKNOWLEDGMENTS

It was a surprise for me to discover that the process of writing a horror novel was as terrifying (if not more so) than the experience of reading one. My most sincere gratitude to everyone who came along for the ride.

First and foremost, thank you to Jodi Reamer for your unwavering faith, your vision for my career, and your enthusiasm for this dark and twisty story. Also, I must thank you for encouraging me to read *The Fifth Child* while I was pregnant with my first. Thanks, too, Alec Shane, for your swift and sound support.

Elizabeth Law is yet again responsible for all of the very best parts of this book. She is a unique blend of irreverence, brilliance, and loyalty—a true advocate for her authors. I'd say that every writer should have the chance to work with her in his or her lifetime, but selfishly, I'd prefer not to have to share.

Infinite thanks to Alison Weiss, always a wise, calming presence, but also exactly the right keen, clever, and capable eye at exactly the most critical time in this editorial process. What would this book be without your insight?

I'm indebted to the extended Egmont USA team: Andrea Cascardi, Regina Griffin, Bonnie Cutler, and Gordon Vanderkamp. Thank you for making me feel like such a valued member of the Egmont family!

Melissa Walker, Lynn Weingarten, and Nova Ren Suma—where to begin? Thank you for accepting my manic communiqués, and for alternately talking me down and propping me up. You are my goddess muses.

To Gwenda Bond and Katie Sise, thank you for early reads. To the Last Mondays Writing Group: Sarah MacLane, Morgan Baden, Lauren Mechling, Sara Lyle, and Lisa Chambers—thank you for reading this book so, so many times and offering so much brilliance amidst the wine and gossip.

To Libba Bray: thank you for politely allowing me to "explain" to you how plotting works. And for not laughing (too hard) when I realized with horror that I was trying to *explain to LIBBA BRAY how plotting works.*

Meg Leder, Jill Gottlieb, and Nancy Lambert—our early upstate retreat was the start of it all. I'm glad the house wasn't (evidently) haunted.

Adele Griffin, thank you for saying some of the nicest things I've ever heard about my work from someone who wasn't related to me. And for your boundless hospitality, which gave the work a much-needed jumpstart. Also, for the conversation with Jenny Han about mortally wounded guinea pigs, which did make its way into this book oh-so-covertly.

To the VCFA-sters and the Kindling Words-sters: Mariana Baer, Rita Williams-Garcia, Laura Ruby, Sarah

Aronson, Shawn Stout, Gene Brenek, Mikki Knudsen, Varian Johnson, Louise Hawes, Tim Wynn-Jones, Leda Schubert, Trent Reedy, Jill Santopolo, Margo Rabb, Rachel Wilson, Sara Zarr. You are all divine vessels of creative beauty. Mwah!

To the masters: Stephen King, Shirley Jackson, Mary Shelley, Sam Raimi, George Romero, Wes Craven, Joss Whedon. Yes, please, more, thank you. (* genuflects *)

To my darling, sprawling family: Dad, Dave, Lily, Josh, Elizabeth, Len, and Fleur—how does one author wind up with so many viable writing-retreat options? Love, love, love.

To dearest Mazzy, so terrifyingly brave. You may not read this book until you are 40.

To Noah, love of my life, thank you for believing in ghosts. And in me.

And finally, to my mother, Carmen Ostow, who took me to the library every single Saturday morning when I was growing up. She always pretended not to see me ducking out of the children's section and hiding in the grown-up stacks to read *The Shining* in weekly installments. I love you. This book, especially, is yours.